Maigret and the Informer

Maigret and the Informer

Georges Simenon

Translated from the French by Lyn Moir

Originally published in England under the title *Maigret and the Flea*

A Helen and Kurt Wolff Book

Harcourt Brace Jovanovich, Inc. New York

First American edition 1973
Originally published in French under the title
Maigret et l'Indicateur
ISBN: 0-15-155140-5
Library of Congress Catalog Card Number: 72-91839
Printed in the United States of America
B C D E

Maigret and the Informer

1

When the telephone rang and Maigret groaned with displeasure, he had not the slightest idea what time it might be. He didn't think of looking at the alarm clock. He was coming out of a deep sleep and still felt a weight on his chest.

Barefoot, walking as if asleep, he went to the telephone.

"Hello. . . ."

He did not notice that it was not he but his wife who had turned on one of the bedside lamps.

"Is that you, Chief?"

He did not recognize the voice right away.

"Lucas here. I'm on night duty. I've just had a call from the 18th *arrondissement.*"

"Well?"

"They've found the body of a murdered man on the sidewalk on Avenue Junot."

It was right at the top of the Butte Montmartre, not far from Place du Tertre.

"I'm calling you because of the identity of the dead man. It's Maurice Marcia, the proprietor of the Sardine."

A truly Parisian restaurant on Rue Fontaine.

"What was he doing on Avenue Junot?"

"He doesn't seem to have been killed there. They got the impression at first sight that he had been put there after he was already dead."

"I'm on my way."

"Do you want me to send you a car?"

"Yes."

Madame Maigret, still in bed, was looking at him, but now she got up and poked around with her feet to find her slippers.

"I'll make you a cup of coffee."

It had been a bad evening, or rather, too good an evening. It was the Maigrets' turn to have the Pardons in. There was an unspoken agreement between them, consolidated over the years.

Once a month Doctor Pardon and his wife had the Maigrets to dinner in their apartment on Boulevard Voltaire. Two weeks later it would be their turn to go to dinner on Boulevard Richard-Lenoir.

The women would take advantage of the occasion to put on a great spread and to exchange recipes, while the men would gossip idly, drinking Alsatian gin or raspberry brandy.

The dinner had been particularly successful. Madame Maigret had made a guinea-hen pie, and the superintendent had brought out of his cellar one of the last bottles of an old Châteauneuf du Pape he had once bought a case of, marked down, when he was on Rue Drouot.

The wine was exceptionally good, and the two men hadn't left a drop. How many liqueur glasses of brandy had they had afterward? At any rate, suddenly awakened at two o'clock in the morning, Maigret did not feel at his best.

He knew Maurice Marcia. Everyone in Paris knew him. When he was still a detective, he had had the man, not at that time a respectable character, in his office for questioning.

Later on, he and Madame Maigret had sometimes dined on Rue Fontaine, where the cooking was first class.

She brought him his cup of coffee when he was almost dressed.

"Is it important?"

"There's likely to be a scandal."

"Someone well known?"

"Monsieur Maurice, that's what everyone calls him. His real name is Maurice Marcia."

"Of the Sardine?"

He nodded.

"He's been murdered?"

"Looks like it. I'd better go and see for myself."

He sipped his coffee and filled his pipe. Then he opened the window a little to see what the weather was like. It was still raining, such a fine rain and so slow that it was invisible except in the halos of the street lights.

"Are you taking your raincoat?"

"It's not worth it. It's too warm."

It was only May, a May that had been superb. A storm had appeared and changed the weather, and a sort of mist that had lasted for twenty-four hours still remained from it.

"I'll see you when you get back."

"You know, your guinea hens were marvelous."

"Not too heavy?"

He decided not to answer that question, since he could still feel them sitting on his stomach.

A small black car was waiting at the door for him.

"Avenue Junot."

"What number?"

"You'll probably see a crowd hanging around."

The streets were as black and shiny as if they had been lacquered. There was almost no traffic. It took them only a few minutes to get to Montmartre, but not the Montmartre of night clubs and tourists. Avenue Junot was nearly at the edge of that hive of activity, mostly lined by villas which artists who had begun on the Butte and had remained faithful to it had had built there after they had become prosperous.

They saw a crowd on the right-hand sidewalk and, in spite of the hour, there were lights in the windows and people in their nightclothes leaning out.

The local superintendent had already arrived, a small, thin, shy man who rushed toward Maigret.

"I'm glad you're here, Superintendent. It's a case that is bound to cause a scandal."

"Are you sure of his identity?"

"Here is his wallet."

He held out a black crocodile wallet that contained

only an identity card, a driver's license, and a note pad with some telephone numbers written on it.

"No money?"

"A whole bundle of notes, three or four thousand francs, I haven't counted them, in his hip pocket."

"No weapon?"

"A Smith and Wesson that hasn't been used recently."

Maigret went over to the body, and it seemed strange to him to be looking down on Monsieur Maurice like that. He was wearing a dinner jacket, as he did every evening, and a bloodstain spread widely over his shirt front.

"No traces of blood on the ground?"

"No."

"Who found the body?"

"I did," said a soft voice behind him.

It was an old man whose white hair formed a halo around his head. Maigret thought he recognized a rather well-known painter, but he couldn't remember his name.

"I live in the villa just across the way. I often wake up at night and find it difficult to go back to sleep."

He was wearing pajamas, over which he had slipped an old raincoat. On his feet were red slippers.

"When that happens I go to the window and look out. Avenue Junot is quiet and deserted. There's practically no car traffic. I was surprised to see a black-and-white shape on the sidewalk and I came down to see what it was. I called the police station. These men appeared in a car with its siren blaring, and the windows filled up with people trying to see what was going on."

There were about twenty people, passers-by and neighbors in their nightclothes, looking at the body and the little group of officials. A local doctor said:

"There's nothing more for me to do here. I can assure

you he's quite dead. The rest is the medical examiner's affair."

"I have called him," the local superintendent said. "And I have informed the Public Prosecutor's Office."

And, in fact, a deputy public prosecutor was getting out of a car, accompanied by his clerk. He was surprised to find Maigret on the spot.

"Do you think it's an important case?"

"I'm afraid so. Do you know Maurice Marcia?"

"No."

"You've never had dinner at the Sardine?"

"No."

He had to explain to him that one was as likely to find the top levels of society and of the arts there as the top levels of the crime world.

Doctor Bourdet, the medical examiner who had replaced Doctor Paul, got out of a taxi grumbling, shook hands with everyone, and said to Maigret:

"Ah! You're here too!"

He leaned over the body and examined the wound with the aid of a flashlight, which he took from his bag.

"Just one bullet, if I'm not mistaken, but large caliber and fired at point-blank range."

"When do you think he died?"

"If he was brought here right away, the crime must have been committed about midnight. Let's say between midnight and one o'clock. I'll tell you more after the autopsy."

Maigret went over to Véliard, an inspector of the 18th *arrondissement*, who was keeping modestly in the background.

"Did you know Monsieur Maurice?"

"By reputation and by sight."

"Does he live in the district?"

"I'm almost certain he lives in the 9th *arrondissement*. In the vicinity of Rue Ballu."

"He didn't have a mistress around here?"

It was odd, in fact, for someone with a body on his hands to come from another district to deposit it in peaceful Avenue Junot.

"I think I would have heard about it. Someone who must know is Inspector Louis of the 9th *arrondissement,* who knows the area around Pigalle like the back of his hand."

Maigret shook hands all around and got into the little black car just as a reporter arrived, a tall redhead, his hair standing on end.

"Monsieur Maigret . . ."

"Not now. Ask the inspector or the local superintendent."

And he said to his driver: "Rue Ballu."

He had kept the dead man's identity card as a matter of habit and he added, after consulting it:

"21 bis."

It was a rather large private house, like several others in the street, and it had been converted into apartments. To the right of the door was a brass plate with the name of a dentist and the note "2nd floor." On the third floor was a neurologist.

The bell woke the concierge.

"Monsieur Maurice Marcia, please."

"Monsieur Maurice is never in at this time. Not before four in the morning."

"What about Madame Marcia?"

"I think she's back. I don't think she'll see you. Try anyway, if you think it's worth your while. First floor, the door on the left. They have the whole floor, but the door on the right is blocked up."

The staircase was wide, covered with a thick carpet. The

walls were of yellowish marble. There was no name on the door at the left, and Maigret rang the bell.

At first there was silence. Then he rang again and at last he heard footsteps inside. Through the door a woman's voice, thick with sleep, asked:

"Who is it?"

"Superintendent Maigret."

"My husband isn't here. Go to the restaurant on Rue Fontaine."

"Your husband isn't there either."

"Have you been there?"

"No. But I know he isn't there."

"Just a moment while I put something on."

When she opened the door she was wearing a golden-yellow housecoat over a white silk nightdress. She was young, much younger than her husband, who was a few years older than Maigret, approximately sixty or sixty-two.

She looked at him indifferently, hardly curious.

"Why do you want my husband at this hour of the night?"

She was tall, very blonde, with the thin supple body of a model or a chorus girl. She could be only thirty at the most.

"Come in."

She opened the door of a big living room, where she put on the light.

"When did you last see your husband?"

"At about eight o'clock, like any other day, when he left for Rue Fontaine."

"Did he go by car?"

"Of course not. It's only five hundred yards away."

"Does he never take the car to go there?"

"Only when it's pouring."

"Do you go with him?"

"No."

"Why not?"

"Because it's not my place. What would I do there?"

"So you spend all your evenings here?"

She seemed surprised by these questions but did not take exception to them. Nor did she show much curiosity.

"Almost all. I go to the movies sometimes, like everybody else."

"You don't go in and say hello to him in passing?"

"No."

"Did you go to the movies this evening?"

"No."

"Did you go out?"

"No. Only to walk the dog. Since it was raining, I only stayed outside a few minutes."

"At what time?"

"About eleven. Perhaps a little later."

"You didn't meet anyone you knew?"

"No. What's behind all these questions and why are you interested in what I was doing this evening?"

"Your husband is dead."

She stared at him. Her eyes were a pale blue, quite expressive. At the same time she opened her mouth as if to cry out but her throat constricted and she put her hand to her breast. She fumbled for a handkerchief in the pocket of her housecoat and hid her face in it.

Maigret waited, motionless, seated in an uncomfortable Louis XV chair.

"Was it his heart?" she asked at last, crumpling the handkerchief into a ball.

"What do you mean?"

"He didn't like anyone to talk about it, but he had a heart ailment and he was seeing Professor Jardin."

"He didn't die of heart failure. He was killed."

"Where?"

"I don't know. His body was taken afterward to Avenue Junot and dropped on the sidewalk."

"It's not possible. He didn't have any enemies."

"He must have had at least one, since he was murdered."

She stood up in one movement.

"Where is he now?"

"At the Medico-Legal Institute."

"Do you mean they're going to . . ."

"To perform an autopsy, yes. It is inevitable."

A little white dog came slowly from the hall and rubbed itself against its mistress's legs. She seemed not to notice it.

"What did they tell you at the restaurant?"

"I haven't been there yet. What could they say?"

"They could say why he left the Sardine so early. He's always the last one there, and it's he who locks up before counting the takings."

"Have you worked there?"

"No. It's a restaurant, strictly for food. There are no song or dance numbers."

"You were a dancer?"

"Yes."

"You don't dance any more?"

"Not since I got married."

"How long have you been married?"

"Four years."

"Where did you meet him?"

"At the Sardine. I was dancing at the Canary. When I didn't finish too late I would sometimes go there and have a bite to eat."

"And that's how he noticed you?"

"Yes."

12

"Were you a hostess too?"

She winced.

"It depends on what you mean by that. If a customer invited us, we wouldn't refuse to drink a bottle of champagne with him, but that was all."

"Did you have a lover?"

"Why do you ask me that?"

"Because I'm trying to find out who could have a grudge against your husband."

"I didn't have one at the time I met him."

"Was he a jealous man?"

"Very."

"What about you?"

"Don't you think, Superintendent, it's hardly the moment to question a woman when she has just learned that her husband is dead?"

"Have you got a car of your own?"

"Maurice gave me an Alfa-Romeo recently."

"What about him? What kind of car did he have?"

"A Bentley."

"Did he drive?"

"He had a chauffeur, but he sometimes drove himself."

"I'm sorry I had to bother you. Unfortunately, it's my job."

He got up, sighing. Silence reigned in the big living room with a sumptuous Chinese rug occupying the center spot.

She led him to the door.

"I may perhaps have other questions to ask you in the next few days. Would you rather that I called you to the Quai des Orfèvres or that I came to see you here?"

"Here."

"Thank you."

She answered him with a curt good evening.

His stomach still felt heavy, his head thick.

"Take me to the Sardine, Rue Fontaine."

There were still several impressive cars in front of the restaurant, and a doorman in livery was walking up and down on the sidewalk. Maigret went in and breathed the cool air, for the room was air-conditioned.

The headwaiter, a man he knew well, Raoul Comitat, rushed up to him.

"A table, Monsieur Maigret?"

"No."

"If you want to see the boss, he isn't here."

The headwaiter was bald and pasty-faced.

"That's odd, isn't it?" Maigret remarked.

"It almost never happens."

The restaurant, which was spacious, had twenty or twenty-five tables. The beams in the ceiling were exposed, the walls paneled in old oak to three-quarters of their height. Everything was heavy, rich, without most of the tastelessness that almost always goes with the rustic style.

It was after three o'clock. There were only about ten people left, mostly actors, legitimate stage and variety, who were dining quietly.

"When did Marcia leave?"

"I couldn't say exactly, but it must have been around midnight."

"That didn't surprise you."

"Oh, it did! I doubt if it has happened three or four times in twenty years. Besides, you know him. I've served you and your wife several times. He is always in a dinner jacket, his hands behind his back. He looks as if he doesn't move, and yet he sees everything. You think he is in the dining room, and he is already in the kitchens or in his office."

"Did he tell you he was going to come back?"

"He just said, 'See you shortly.'

"We were near the cloakroom. Yvonne handed him his hat. I reminded him that it was raining and advised him to take his raincoat, which was hanging on one of the hooks.

" 'It's not worth it. I'm not going far.' "

"Did he seem preoccupied?"

"His expression was difficult to read."

"Was he angry?"

"Certainly not."

"He hadn't had a phone call just before going out?"

"You'll have to ask at the desk. All the phone calls are taken by the cashier. But tell me, what's behind these questions?"

"Because he was shot dead, and his body has been found lying on the sidewalk on Avenue Junot."

The headwaiter's features stiffened and his lower lip began to tremble slightly.

"It's not possible," he murmured to himself. "Who could have done that? I can't think of even one enemy. He was basically a good man, very happy, very proud of his success. Was there a fight?"

"No. He was killed somewhere else and taken to Avenue Junot, probably in a car. Didn't you tell me he was wearing a hat when he went out?"

"Yes."

There was no hat on the ground on Avenue Junot.

"I have some questions to ask the cashier."

The headwaiter rushed to a table where the customers were asking for their bill. It was ready and he put it on a plate, half covered with a napkin.

The cashier was a small, dark girl, very thin, with lovely dark eyes.

"I am Superintendent Maigret."

15

"I know."

"There's no point in hiding it from you any longer. Your boss has just been murdered."

"So that's why you looked so conspiratorial when you were talking with Raoul. I . . . I'm stunned. He was there not long ago, right where you're standing."

"Did he have any phone calls?"

"Just one, a few minutes before he went out."

"From a man? A woman?"

"That's just what I wondered. It could have been one or the other, a man with a slightly high voice or a woman with a rather deep voice."

"Had you heard that voice before?"

"No. He asked to speak to Monsieur Maurice."

"Is that what they called him?"

"Yes. Like all his friends. I asked who was speaking, and he answered:

" 'He'll know.'

"When I looked up, Monsieur Maurice was standing in front of me.

" 'Is that for me? Who is it?'

" 'No name.'

"He frowned and held out his hand for the phone.

" 'Who's speaking, please?'

"Of course, I couldn't hear what the person at the other end was saying.

" 'What's that? I can't hear you very well. . . . What? . . . Are you sure? . . . If I ever catch you . . .'

"The person must have been calling from a telephone booth, because he put more money in. I recognized the sound.

" 'I know where that is as well as you do.'

"He hung up suddenly. He was on his way to the door

when he turned around and went to his office, behind the kitchens."

"Does he often go there?"

"Seldom during the evening. When he comes in he goes there to look over the mail. In the evenings, after we close, I take him the money and we check it together."

"Does the money stay here until the next day?"

"No. He takes it away in a brief case that is used for only that purpose."

"I suppose he carries a gun?"

"He takes his gun out of the drawer and puts it in his pocket."

That night Monsieur Maurice had not been carrying the money and yet he had gone back to his office for his gun.

"Is there another gun that remains here?"

"No. As far as I know, he has only that one."

"Would you show me his office?"

"Just a moment. . . ."

She held out a note to Raoul Comitat.

"This way."

They went along a hallway with green-painted walls. On the left, a glass panel gave a view of the kitchen, where four men appeared to be tidying up.

"Here it is. I suppose you have the right to go in."

The office was simple, furnished without any ostentation. There were three good leather armchairs, an Empire desk in mahogany, a safe behind it, and shelves with books and magazines.

"Is there any money in the safe?"

"No. Only the books. We could do without it. It was there when Monsieur Maurice bought the restaurant and he never had it taken away."

"Where is the gun usually kept?"

17

"In the drawer on the right."

"Does Madame Marcia call her husband often?"

"Hardly ever."

"She didn't call this evening?"

"No. The call would have come through me."

"What about him? Doesn't he call her?"

"Rarely. I don't remember the last time he did. It must have been before last Christmas."

"Thank you."

Maigret was feeling the weight of his tiredness and he let himself drop onto the back seat of the little black car.

"Boulevard Richard-Lenoir."

The rain had stopped but the ground was still shiny, and the sky was beginning to grow lighter in the east.

He felt vaguely that there was something wrong in this case. True, Monsieur Maurice was no saint. He had had a fairly stormy youth and he had been sentenced several times for procuring.

Then, when he was about thirty, he moved up in the world, becoming the proprietor of a brothel which at that time was one of the best known in Paris, on Rue de Hanovre.

The brothel wasn't registered in his name. He spent a good part of his afternoons at the races. When he wasn't there, he could most probably be found, along with other shady characters, playing cards in a *bistrot* on Rue Victor-Massé.

Some people called him the Judge. They said that when a dispute came up among people of the underworld it was he who made the final decision.

He was a good-looking man, dressed by the best tailors, and he wore only silk underwear. He was married and already lived on Rue Ballu.

He grew plumper with age and that gave him an added dignity.

Oh! Maigret had forgotten to ask the cashier if the man who had phoned had had an accent. That might be important at some time.

For the moment he was at a loss. He remembered something Maurice Marcia had said at one of their last meetings at the Quai des Orfèvres. Marcia was not there on his own account, but his bartender appeared to have taken part in a holdup at a branch of one of the big banks, at Puteaux.

"What's your opinion of this Freddy?"

The bartender was called Freddy Strazzia and came from Piedmont.

"I think he's a good bartender."

"Do you think he's honest?"

"Well, Superintendent, it depends on what you mean by that. There's honest and honest. When we met, when we were both what you might call beginners at our trades, I didn't consider myself a dishonest man. Which wasn't your opinion, or that of the judges.

"Little by little, I changed. One might say that I have spent forty years of my life becoming an honest man. Well, it's the way it is with converts. They say they are the most devout. So, honest men who have become so by their own efforts are more meticulous than others.

"You're asking me if Freddy is honest. I wouldn't stake my life on it, but what I am certain of is that he isn't such a fool as to have anything to do with such a badly organized affair as that."

The car had stopped in front of his house. He thanked the driver and went upstairs slowly, puffing a little. He could hardly wait to get into bed and close his eyes.

"Are you tired?"

"I've had all I can take."

Less than ten minutes later he was asleep.

It was almost eleven o'clock when he began to show signs of life, and Madame Maigret hurried to bring him a cup of coffee.

"Goodness!" he exclaimed. "The sun's shining again."

"Was it this case on Rue Fontaine that kept you out last night?"

"How did you know?"

"From the radio. From the papers. They say that Monsieur Maurice was a real Parisian personality."

"Let's say a character," he corrected.

"Did you know him?"

"Ever since I started in the Criminal Police."

"Do you understand why they dumped his body on Avenue Junot?"

"So far I haven't a clue. And the greatest puzzle is why Marcia still had his gun in his pocket."

"Why?"

"I'm astonished that he didn't shoot first. He must have been taken by surprise."

He sat down in his armchair in his dressing gown and dialed the number of the Criminal Police.

At that time Lucas, who had been on night duty, was sound asleep in bed. It was Janvier who answered.

"Not too tired, Chief?"

"No. I'm all right now. Do you know what's been going on?"

"From the papers and from the reports that have just come in, particularly that of the police station in the 18th *arrondissement*. And I've had a phone call from Doctor Bourdet."

"What does he say?"

"The shot was fired from a distance of about three to five feet. The gun is probably a short-barreled revolver, a .32 or a .38. He sent the bullet to the lab. As for poor Marcia, his death was almost instantaneous; he had an internal hemorrhage."

"So he didn't bleed very much?"

"Very little."

"Did he have a heart defect?"

"Bourdet didn't mention it to me. Do you want to ask him?"

"I'm going to do that myself. I'll be at the office early this afternoon. If anything new comes up, no matter what, call me."

A few minutes later he had Doctor Bourdet on the line.

"I suppose you're just getting up," he said to Maigret. "I was working until nine o'clock this morning and now they've brought me another customer, a woman this time. . . ."

"Tell me, apart from the wound, did you note anything special, any sign of any illness?"

"No. He was a healthy man, in very good shape for his age."

"Nothing wrong with his heart?"

"As far as I can judge, his heart was in good condition."

"Thank you, Doctor."

Hadn't Line, Marcia's blonde wife, spoken to him of Professor Jardin, saying that her husband had consulted him from time to time? He telephoned the professor's house and then the hospital, where he found him.

"I'm sorry to trouble you, Professor. This is Superintendent Maigret. I believe one of your patients died a sudden death last night. I mean Maurice Marcia."

"The restaurant owner in Montmartre? I've only seen him once. I believe he was thinking of taking out life insurance, and before the official examination he wanted to see a doctor of his own choosing."

"The result?"

"The heart was in perfect condition."

"Thank you."

"Well," Madame Maigret asked, "was he ill?"

"No."

"Why did his wife tell you. . . ?"

"I don't know that any more than you do. Would you give me another cup of coffee?"

"What would you like for lunch?"

He could still feel the heaviness he had had in his stomach during the night.

"Some ham, boiled potatoes lightly fried in oil, and a green salad."

"Is that all? Couldn't you digest the guinea hen?"

"I digested it all right, but I think Pardon and I went a bit heavy on the brandy. And that's not counting the wine. . . ."

He got up sighing and lit his first pipe, then stood in front of the open window. He hadn't been there more than ten minutes when the telephone rang.

"Hello, Chief. Janvier here. I've just had a visit from Inspector Louis of the 9th *arrondissement*. It was you he wanted to see. He appears to have something interesting to say to you. He's wondering if you could see him early this afternoon."

"Tell him to come to my office at two o'clock."

With Louis, one never knew. He was a strange man. He was about forty-five, he must have been a widower for fifteen years, and he always wore black from head to foot, as if he were still in mourning for his wife. And, in his *arrondissement,* his colleagues called him the Widower behind his back.

One never saw him laugh or joke. When he was on desk duty he worked nonstop. Since he didn't smoke, he didn't even have to light a pipe or a cigarette.

Most of the time he was on street duty, preferably at night. He was probably the man in Paris who knew the Pigalle district best.

He rarely spoke to a prostitute or a pimp without good reason, and they would watch him go by with some alarm. He lived alone in the apartment in which he had lived with his wife, on the other side of the boulevard, at the bottom of Rue Lepic. He had even been born in the district. He could often be seen doing his marketing.

He knew the pedigree of all the male prostitutes of the area, the story of all the girls.

He would go into the bars, never taking his hat off. He would invariably order a quarter-bottle of Vichy. That way he could stay a long time, watching. Sometimes he would speak to the bartender.

"I didn't know Francis was back from Toulon."

"Are you sure?"

"He's just seen me and slunk off to the men's room."

"I haven't seen him. That surprises me, because he usually comes and talks to me when he is in Paris."

"That's probably because of me."

"Whom was he with?"

"Madeleine."

"That's his old girl friend."

He never took notes, and yet all the surnames, the Christian names, the nicknames of all those men and women were filed methodically in his head.

Rue Fontaine was in his district. He must know more about Monsieur Maurice than Maigret or anyone else. Besides, he wouldn't have come to the Quai des Orfévres by chance, for he was a shy man.

He knew that he would never get higher than inspector and he was wisely content with that, doing his job as best he could. Having no other passion in life, he devoted his life to it.

"I'm going down to buy some ham."

He watched her out of the window, as she walked toward Rue Servan. He was glad to have a wife like her and smiled with satisfaction.

How long had Inspector Louis been married before his wife had been run over by a bus? Only a few years at the most, since he had been thirty at the time. He had been looking out the window, as Maigret was at that moment, and the accident had occurred under his very eyes.

Maigret touched wood, an unusual thing for him to do, and stayed by the window until he saw his wife cross the boulevard again and come into the building.

Louis was the inspector's surname. Maigret had once thought of getting him to join his group, but he was such a lugubrious character that the atmosphere of the inspectors' office would have been affected.

In the office in the 9th *arrondissement*, where there were only three inspectors and a trainee, they fixed it so that Louis worked outside as much as possible.

"Poor man!"

"Are you talking to yourself?"

"What did I say?"

"You said 'Poor man.' Were you thinking about Marcia?"

"No. I was thinking about a man whose wife died fifteen years ago and who still wears mourning for her."

"He isn't all in black, is he? Nobody does that any more."

"He does. He doesn't care what people think. Some people, meeting him for the first time, take him for a priest and call him 'Father.' "

"Aren't you going to shave? And have a bath?"

"I will. But I feel delightfully lazy."

He finished his pipe before going into the bathroom.

2

The windows in Maigret's office had been opened again to the breezes outside and to the noise of cars and buses on the Pont Saint-Michel.

Inspector Louis was sitting on the edge of the chair that the superintendent had pointed out to him. His movements were slow, almost solemn, in keeping with his black clothing, which stood out even more on this spring day.

"Thank you for seeing me, Superintendent."

His skin was fine and very white, almost a woman's skin, and his thick black mustache stood out against it. His lips were red, as if they had been made up, and yet there was nothing effeminate about him.

He must have been the timid boy in the class, the one who blushed and stammered as soon as the teacher spoke to him.

"I would like to ask you something."

"Please do."

"Is it the inspectors of the 18th *arrondissement* who will investigate the case, since the body was found on Avenue Junot?"

Maigret had to think before he answered.

"They will certainly question potential witnesses, check up on a car that stopped on the avenue in the middle of the night, and question the old painter who alerted the police, as well as the other neighbors."

"But what about the rest?"

"As you know, it's a Criminal Division affair. Which doesn't prevent us from accepting, or even seeking, help from local inspectors. You know Montmartre very well, don't you?"

"I was born there and I still live there."

"You have been in contact with Maurice Marcia."

"With him and with his employees."

He blushed. He was having to make a great effort to say all that he had promised himself he would say.

"Listen, I almost always work at night. I've got to know everybody. In Pigalle they are used to me. I exchange a few words with this man or that. I go into the bars and cabarets where, without waiting for me to order anything, they give me a quarter-bottle of Vichy."

"I imagine that, since you have come to see me, you have an idea about Marcia's murder."

27

"I think I know who killed him."

Maigret pulled gently on his pipe, a little taken aback, observing the other man with curiosity, even with a certain fascination.

"Are your suspicions based on anything?"

"Yes and no."

He was embarrassed and didn't dare look the superintendent in the face.

"I had a phone call this morning."

"An anonymous call?"

"More or less. I've been getting phone calls from the same person for years."

"A man or a woman?"

"A man. He has always refused to tell me his name. Whenever anything fairly mysterious happens in Montmartre, he calls me, and he always begins by saying:

" 'It's me.'

"I recognize his voice. I know he calls from a phone booth and he doesn't waste any time, tells me only the essentials. For example:

" 'They're planning an armed robbery in the La Chapelle district. It's Coglia's gang.' "

"Coglia still has several years to go in prison," objected Maigret.

"His old accomplices keep things going."

"Is your anonymous informer never wrong?"

"Never."

"Doesn't he ask you for money?"

"No. Nor does he ask me to turn a blind eye on any more or less illegal activities."

Maigret was growing interested.

"And he called you this morning?"

"Yes. At eight o'clock, just before I went out to do my

marketing. I live alone and I have to do my marketing myself."

"What exactly did he say to you?"

"Monsieur Maurice was murdered by one of the Mori brothers."

"Is that all?"

"That's all. Do you know the Mori brothers, Manuel and Jo?"

"We've been trying to catch them red-handed for two years. Up to now we haven't been able to prove anything against them."

"I'm watching them too. They don't live together. Manuel, the elder brother, has a bourgeois, even luxury apartment on Square La Bruyère."

A stone's throw from the Sardine.

"Jo, who is twenty-nine, has a suite in the Hôtel des Iles, on Avenue Trudaine.

"But you must have all this information in your files. They have a wholesale fruit and vegetable business on Rue du Caire. Either one or the other is there every day. It's a long building that opens directly from the street."

"Did they have any dealings with Monsieur Maurice?"

"They sometimes had dinner with him. They're not the only rogues to go to the Sardine."

"Did Marcia ever help them?"

"I don't think so. He had become frightened and held tight to his respectability."

"Which of the two brothers did your anonymous caller mean?"

"I don't know, but I will certainly be getting another phone call before long. That's why I asked to see you."

"Do you want to help with the investigation?"

"I would like to assist somehow, officially, in my own

way. I have never done anything outside my normal work. You may trust me. I promise to keep you in the picture about anything I find out."

"Do you know the Mori brothers well?"

"I see them in several bars. Manuel had a very beautiful mistress from Martinique."

"What has happened to her?"

"She dances and sings in a *boîte* for tourists."

"Who's replaced her?"

"Nobody. I always see him alone or with his brother. The brother's set up with a girl from the provinces. Her name's Marcelle and she's twenty-two."

"You don't think she could be the weak link in the chain?"

"She's crazy about Jo Mori and she has a strong character."

"Do you think she knows what the two brothers are up to?"

"I don't know how far they take her into their confidence. And I have never seen them around with people who could be their accomplices when they pull off a job."

There had been ten robberies, all done in the same way, with an identical technique. It was always a château or big property in the provinces, within a radius of about a hundred and twenty miles from Paris.

The thieves were well informed. They knew what articles of value, what pictures, what pieces of furniture were to be found in the buildings. They also knew if the proprietors were away and how many people were guarding the properties.

They operated noiselessly, breaking no windows. In less than an hour, those things which would be easy to sell would be removed. So they had at least one truck at their disposal.

Now, the Mori brothers had two trucks which they used in their fruit business. As it happened, it was two years since they had started their wholesale business.

Manuel had previously worked for a buyer in Les Halles. Jo had spent three years in an architect's office.

But where were the proceeds of the burglaries stored afterward? They probably remained near Paris, in a villa or a house rented under another name.

"Who could watch over the stuff?"

"I couldn't swear to it, but I think I know. The Moris' mother."

"Do you know her?"

"I've never seen her. I know she exists. She used to live in Arles with her family. When they came to Paris, she stayed a few years longer in the Midi with her daughter. She got married and lives in Marseilles."

Thus, over many years, Inspector Louis had worked alone, patiently, without having recourse to the complicated system of the official police force.

"How do you know all that?"

"I watch. I listen. I have contacts in different places, people whom I can sometimes help. . . ."

"What became of Mother Mori?"

"She sold her house in Arles, with all the furniture, and she hasn't been seen again."

"I expect you have searched the countryside all around Paris."

"I do that on Sundays or on my days off."

"You haven't found anything?"

"Not yet."

He blushed again, as if ashamed of his confidence in himself.

"What do you know about Madame Marcia?"

"You mean the present one? Because there was one before, with whom he lived more than twenty years. They were a very close couple. True, he had picked her out of the gutter, but he had turned her into a bourgeoise. When she died of cancer, he was very upset, and for several months he was not the same man."

There had been a time, when he was still young, when Maigret had pounded the beat, in the streets, in the stations, the métro, the department stores. At that time he also had known all the shady characters of Paris.

Now he had been shut up in an office, and his chief was shocked when he went to interview a suspect at his home, or when he ferreted around outside.

"Where did he find his second wife, Line, the one he was living with now?"

"She worked as a dancer at the Tabarin, and more recently at the Canary. I think that's where he met her. In spite of her profession, she was a quiet girl, not showily dressed, and it seems she never went with the customers. She's a woman of some education."

"You're not going to tell me where she comes from, or where her parents live, or how long she stayed in school?"

Inspector Louis blushed once more.

"She was born in Brussels, where her father works in a bank. She went to school until she was eighteen and then she worked at the same bank. She went to Paris to be with a young man, a painter, who hoped to make his fortune here. He didn't succeed as quickly as he had hoped. Line took a job as a salesgirl in a shop on the Grands Boulevards.

"Her painter dropped her and she went to the Tabarin, where she started by being part of the tableau. . . ."

Maigret had known the inspector for years. Though they would meet from time to time, they had little contact with each other. For a long time he had considered him a pompous nonentity; then he had realized that, on the contrary, he was an intelligent man.

Now he was looking at him almost as if awe-struck.

"Do you know as much about many people in Montmartre?"

"Well, you know, it mounts up over the years."

"Do you keep files?"

"No. I have it all in my head. I haven't anything else to do, no other interest in life."

Maigret got up and opened the door of the inspectors' room.

"Come in here a minute, Janvier."

And, to the two men:

"I suppose you know each other."

They shook hands.

"We've just been having a long talk, Inspector Louis and I, about Marcia's murder. Any more information on it?"

"Only that a red car stopped for a moment, around one o'clock, about halfway along Avenue Junot."

"Our men are going on with the investigation, of course. But Inspector Louis, who knows several of the people concerned, will work on his own and will keep us up to date with whatever he discovers.

"Do you know the Mori brothers?"

"We suspected them at one time of being the leaders of what they call the château gang."

"Are they still being watched?"

"Not particularly. We only keep track of the places where they go. Jo, the younger one, often goes to the south, to Cavaillon and the district around there, to look for early fruits and vegetables."

"Beginning today, you are to have a watch on them day and night."

"On both of them?"

"On both of them."

"Still because of the château business?"

"No. This time it's murder. Maurice Marcia's murder."

Janvier cast a glum glance at his colleague from the 9th *arrondissement.* He was obviously not very pleased at Inspector Louis's intrusion into this case.

"Is there anyone else to be watched?"

"How about the widow?"

"Do you think . . ."

"I don't think, you know that. I look. We all look."

He shook Inspector Louis by the hand.

"Are you going back to Montmartre?"

"Yes."

"Have you got a car?"

"No."

"I'm going there too. Come along in mine. I'd like you to come with us, Janvier."

Janvier took the wheel. Maigret sat beside him smoking his pipe, and Louis sat by himself in the back seat, rather ill at ease.

He had always dreamed of working directly for the Quai des Orfèvres, and the mission Maigret had given him was like a promotion.

On Rue Notre-Dame-de-Lorette, Janvier asked:

"Where are we going?"

"Farther up. Rue Ballu."

"To Maurice Marcia's?"

"Where shall I drop you?" he asked Louis.

"Anywhere, now that I'm on my home ground."

"In that case I'll let you off here."

"You'll know where to find me. My private number's in the book."

"Thank you for your help."

Louis got out awkwardly and began to walk along the sidewalk with regular steps, not hurrying.

Some minutes later Maigret and Janvier rang the doorbell of the converted house. The concierge opened the door. She was hardly forty and still quite pretty. She looked at them through the glass-paneled door which the superintendent pushed open.

"Have they brought the body back?"

"Not yet, but the men from the undertaker's are upstairs. I think the body will be here by the end of the afternoon."

"This is Inspector Janvier, who is working on the case too. How long has Madame Marcia lived in this house?"

"Since they were married. It must be four years."

"Did they entertain a lot?"

"Hardly at all. As you know, he never came in before three or four in the morning. He would sleep all morning, have his lunch and a siesta, and after that his masseur would come."

"Did he have dinner here?"

"Very rarely. Most of the time he ate in his restaurant."

"With his wife?"

"No. I don't think he liked her to go into the Sardine."

"Why not?"

"I suppose because he was afraid she would meet people he didn't want her to. Don't forget that he was in his sixties and she was barely thirty."

"What did she do during the day?"

"She would give orders to the cook and the maid. She would sometimes go to Fauchon's or some other luxury shop to buy things you don't find around here. Once or twice a week she went to the hairdresser."

"In the center of town?"

"On Rue de Castiglione, I think."

"And in the evenings?"

"She would read or watch television. Before going to bed she would take her dog out for ten minutes or so."

"Didn't she ever go to the movies?"

"Probably she did. Once or twice a week she would stay out all evening."

"Did she never have company?"

"Never."

"Thank you. Is she upstairs?"

"Yes. With her dressmaker."

They did not take the elevator, and they rang the doorbell on the first floor. A young maid with opulent breasts opened the door.

"What do you want?"

"To see Madame Marcia."

"She's busy."

"We'll wait."

"Whom shall I say?"

"The Criminal Police."

"Just a moment."

She left them in the hall and went toward a door at the end. The living-room door was open. The Louis XV furniture had disappeared, as had the big Chinese rug, and men balanced on ladders were fixing black hangings on the walls.

So, they were doing things in the grand manner and the living room was being turned into a mortuary chapel. Obviously, the dressmaker was there about the mourning clothes.

"If you will follow me . . ."

She showed them into a study or library where there were books from floor to ceiling. They were leather-bound volumes which Monsieur Maurice had certainly never read.

The chairs were comfortable. There was a little bar which undoubtedly held a refrigerator and there was nothing lying about on the desk, the fittings of which were in red leather.

In that room the English style had been adopted. A humidor in mahogany inlaid with ivory must have contained expensive Havana cigars. Had these furnishings and things been there when Line first came into the house? Or was it she who had given a certain style to the apartment?

"It's a study in which nobody worked very often," Maigret murmured to Janvier. "If you had seen the furniture in the living room, you would have thought you were in a museum."

"It'll make a fantastic mortuary chapel."

Footsteps approached and they fell silent.

She was wearing a very simple black matte silk dress; on her finger was a diamond ring which she probably never took off. She stopped for a moment, framed in the doorway, and there was a look of surprise on her face. She looked from Maigret to Janvier. Was she surprised by confronting two men instead of one? What importance did she give to that? Did it give a more official character to the interview, in her eyes?

"This is Inspector Janvier, who is one of my chief assistants."

She gave a faint nod.

"You must realize I am very busy."

"So are we, believe me, and we have not come to take up your time for our own pleasure."

All three were standing. Since she did nothing about it, it was Maigret who suggested that they sit down.

"Are you going to keep me for long?"

"I don't think so."

"You could have asked me all the questions you wanted to ask me yesterday. I answered you truthfully. The body will be here at seven this evening."

The superintendent appeared not to have heard her. Looking around him with an appreciative air, he asked:

"Was the furniture in the apartment already here when you came, four years ago?"

"Five," she corrected him. "We had been married almost five years."

"The furniture?"

"It was bought at that time. Before that it was different."

"Less elegant, I suppose."

"Of another kind altogether."

"Which of you suggested changing everything?"

"My husband. He didn't want to see me living in an environment that had for so long been that of his first wife."

"I shan't ask you if the pieces are genuine. I admired the furniture in the living room yesterday."

"They are," she answered ungraciously.

"Did you buy them together?"

"He preferred to visit the antique dealers alone and surprise me. But I don't see how this matter of furniture . . ."

"It has probably nothing to do with your husband's death, but we know through experience that in a case of murder nothing must be neglected. Was your husband very rich?"

"I did not discuss money with him. I only know that his restaurant was profitable and that he took a great deal of trouble to see that it should continue to be so."

"He was very much in love with you."

"What makes you think that?"

"One doesn't decorate an apartment in such a fashion for a woman to whom one is indifferent."

"He loved me."

"I imagine that the marriage took place under the communal-property law."

"That's usual, isn't it?"

"When will the funeral service be?"

"Day after tomorrow, in the Church of Notre-Dame-de-Lorette. After the ceremony the body will be taken to Bandol, where we have a villa, and buried in the cemetery there."

"Will you go to Bandol?"

"Of course."

"Will other friends go there?"

"No. I don't know. That has nothing to do with me."

"Another matter—what is going to happen to the restaurant?"

"It will stay open. Except for the day after tomorrow, the day of the funeral."

"Who will run it after that?"

She hesitated for a moment.

"I will," she said, finally.

"Do you think you have sufficient experience?"

"The staff has worked so long with my husband that the business could run itself."

"Your way of life will be completely changed."

Maigret knew that she was exasperated by all these questions which seemed to be leading nowhere, but he went on, clumsily, as it seemed.

"My way of life is nobody's business as long as I don't break any laws, is that not so?"

"It was just a passing thought. Here you live almost the life of a recluse."

"No one stops me from going out."

"I know. You went to the movies sometimes. But you had no friends, men or women. . . ."

The maid entered hesitatingly.

"These gentlemen are asking if we have any green plants, because the place looks empty."

"Show them the ones on the terrace."

And, to Maigret:

"You can see, I am needed. I'm shocked at your insistence, particularly if you are a friend of my husband's, as you led me to believe yesterday."

"I shall try to disturb you as little as possible."

"I warn you that I have decided not to receive you again."

"I'm sorry about that, because that will oblige me to summon you to the Quai des Orfèvres. Your husband came there often in the past, before he became the proprietor of the Sardine. He didn't have a villa at Bandol either."

"Do you have to remind me of these disagreeable things?"

"No. Unlike you, he had good friends. I was wondering if you don't know some of them. Perhaps he had them to stay, in the summer, at his villa in Bandol. The Mori brothers, for example. . . ."

If she trembled, it was so slightly that he could not be sure.

"Should I know them?"

"That's what I'm asking you. There are two of them, Manuel and Jo. They have a wholesale business on Rue du Caire."

"I don't know either of them."

"They often had dinner at the Sardine."

"Where I never set foot."

"One last question. This apartment is extremely large. Will you go on living here alone?"

"My husband always asked me to, as well as wishing me to keep the restaurant and the house in Bandol.

" 'It'll be as if there is still a part of me there,' he would say."

"Was he expecting what happened to him?"

"Certainly not."

"But he carried a gun in his pocket."

"Only when he was bringing the money home. Everyone who has to carry large sums of money regularly carries a gun."

"By the way, once he got home, where did he put the money?"

"In the safe."

"Where is it?"

"Behind that Delacroix painting which you see to the right of the fireplace."

"Do you know the combination?"

"No. I'll have to call in a specialist, probably from the firm that makes these safes."

"Thank you."

She stood up and he could feel that she was still tense. He felt that she was going over all the questions the superintendent had asked her.

What did they lead to, in fact? Maigret himself would have had difficulty in telling her. He still felt that something was wrong. There were some elements in this case that he did not like.

He went outside again with Janvier, and the sun was still high and hot.

"Do you think she knows more than she's saying, Chief?"

"I'd bet my life on that."

"Do you mean she could be . . . shall we say an accessory?"

"I won't go as far as that, but the story is certainly less clear than she wants to have us believe."

"Where are we going?"

"To Rue Fontaine."

There were no customers at that time, but two of the waiters were setting the table for dinner. Freddy, the bartender, was wiping bottles and put them out on the counter.

It was toward him that the superintendent went.

"Isn't Comitat here?"

"He's having a rest in the boss's office."

"Already?"

"What do you mean?"

"That Monsieur Maurice isn't yet buried and he's already making himself comfortable."

"You're making a mistake Even in Monsieur Maurice's time Raoul used to spend an hour taking a nap in one of the armchairs in the office."

"Did you know the funeral service will be the day after tomorrow?"

"I hadn't been told that yet."

"The restaurant will be closed so that all the staff can go."

"That's the usual thing, isn't it?"

"After that, the body will be buried in Bandol."

"That doesn't surprise me. The boss was born somewhere between Marseilles and Toulon, I don't remember in what village, and he closed the restaurant for a month every year so that he could go to his villa in Bandol."

"Don't you wonder what's going to become of the restaurant?"

"It's all the same to me. There'll be someone to run it. It's a real gold mine."

"Well, from now on your boss isn't going to be a man but a woman."

"You're joking."

"Madame Marcia has decided to take her husband's place."

Freddy made a face, then muttered:

"It's her business, after all."

"Do you know her?"

"I knew her when she was at the Tabarin. I worked there for two years before I came here. She was in the chorus there."

"And what do you think of her?"

"I haven't had much occasion to speak to her. When she came to the bar she would ask for her drink, and that was all. I thought she was a bit snooty. Here in Montmartre we're more used to the friendly type. Still, she had class with it. She didn't come from nowhere, and I wouldn't be surprised if she had had a good education."

"Do the Mori brothers still have dinner here often?"

Freddy saw no harm in the question.

"From time to time. Not regularly. They have to get up early because of their business, you know."

"Are they still friendly with the boss?"

"Monsieur Maurice would sit down for a few minutes at their table, as he would with good customers. And he would sometimes give them an old brandy from his private stock."

"But Madame Marcia never came?"

"Never."

"You don't know why?"

"I suppose because Monsieur Maurice was jealous. She's a pretty girl, if you like that type. There was more than thirty years' difference in their ages."

He looked toward the end of the room.

"Here's Raoul taking up his post."

The headwaiter had seen them and came up to them, holding out his hand to Maigret and then to Janvier.

"Did you come to see me?"

"We hoped to see you, but our visit hasn't any particular reason. I was saying to Freddy that the funeral would be the day after tomorrow at the Church of Notre-Dame-de-Lorette."

"Then we'll close. It would have been more correct for someone to tell me sooner. After all, the whole weight of the business rests on me for the moment. I've been here for sixteen years and she . . ."

He stopped, embarrassed. He had obviously been going to say:

"And she has been sleeping in his bed for only five years."

"Do you know who is going to replace Monsieur Maurice?"

"From the way you ask that question, I can guess. Besides, I already thought about it yesterday. It's she, isn't it?"

"Yes. Do you know her?"

"I saw her at Bandol. The boss knew I was on the coast during the vacation and he invited me to dinner at his villa.

"It would be a good place to end one's days, I can assure you. It's not very big. Nothing flashy. But genuine, substantial stuff. I'm from the Midi too. I know something about antique Provençal furniture. I have rarely seen pieces like Monsieur Maurice's."

He turned to Freddy.

"Haven't you served these gentlemen with anything yet? What will you have?"

"A beer."

"Me too," said Janvier, slightly embarrassed.

And Comitat sighed.

"Still, it'll be funny to have a woman for a boss. It'll be a bit like a brothel, won't it!"

"Some customers will no doubt feel at home."

"All kinds of people come here, you know. Cabinet members, theater people, producers, and even bankers. Lawyers too, and doctors, and, as you have just said, some former criminals."

"Do the Mori brothers still come?"

There was a short silence.

"Occasionally. As far as I'm concerned, I've never liked them very much, particularly Manuel. That boy's a real show-off. He has fantastic cars, and to look at him you'd think he was as rich as Croesus. Well, it's Jo, his brother, who runs the business. Manuel hardly sets foot in Rue du Caire and he spends most of his time playing around Deauville, Le Touquet, and places like that."

"With women?"

"He must have plenty of them, for he's a good-looking boy, but I don't know that he has any serious attachments. It's none of my business. The boss seemed to have a soft spot for him."

"One thing surprises me. Monsieur Maurice seemed to be very much in love and very jealous of his wife. He would leave her alone at home with the cook and the maid. Now, if I've understood correctly what the cashier said to me yesterday, he didn't take the trouble to phone her, not even to say good night."

"How would you know about that?"

"What do you mean? Was the cashier lying?"

"She wasn't lying, but she doesn't know any more about it than I do. The boss would often go to his office after asking for a line to be switched to his phone. So he could call whomever he wanted to."

"Did that happen often?"

"Once or twice an evening."

"Do you think he was calling his wife?"

"He would perhaps tend to other business, but he must have phoned her too."

"And if she hadn't been there?"

The headwaiter looked at him without answering.

"It looks as if that never happened," he murmured a moment later.

And one could guess what he was thinking.

The cashier had taken up her post behind the little counter which was reserved for her and she was getting the cash ready.

"May I have a word with her?"

"Of course, Superintendent."

And, as Maigret wanted to pay for the two beers, Comitat added:

"It's on the house."

"Good evening, mademoiselle."

"Good evening, Superintendent."

"You told me yesterday, or rather this morning, that Monsieur Maurice very rarely asked you to put through a phone call for him."

"That's right."

"And yet he phoned his wife almost every night."

"I don't know anything about that. He would sometimes ask me to switch his phone to an outside line. In that case I couldn't know whom he was calling."

"Was it always at the same time?"

"Never before eleven o'clock. Usually about half past twelve."

"Did he make any out-of-town calls?"

"Occasionally. I know that from the telephone bills, since it's my job to settle the accounts."

"Did he always call the same place?"

"No. The one that came up most often was a little village which I had trouble finding on the map. Les Eglandes, in the Oise."

"Did you know that your new boss is going to be a woman?"

"I thought as much."

"How will that affect you?"

"It's never very pleasant . . . Well, we'll see."

There were now two customers at the bar. Maigret and Janvier got into the car.

"To the Quai, Chief?"

"I'm wondering if I shouldn't go home. I think I'm growing lazy. And it's exhausting to ask questions without knowing where they're leading."

"Do you think Marcia's murder was premeditated?"

"No. Or else it's one of the most extraordinary crimes I've ever come across."

"You keep talking about the Mori brothers."

"Because I've had my eye on them for a long time. It wasn't for nothing that I mentioned the furniture just now, to Madame Marcia's great surprise.

"Maurice was a rough diamond, with no education in the arts. Then, practically from one day to the next, he fills his apartment with genuine antiques which are almost museum pieces."

"The château gang?"

"Why not? There's no lack of taste, at least as far as I know. I intend to have the apartment gone over by an expert. If the furniture and furnishings were bought from antique dealers, there will be receipts somewhere."

"Do you think Line Marcia knows about it?"

"I wouldn't swear she did; on the other hand I wouldn't swear she didn't, either. She took a great deal of trouble to tell us that she had never gone with her husband when he bought the things. . . ."

It was traffic-jam time, and it took them almost three

quarters of an hour to get to Boulevard Richard-Lenoir.

"See you tomorrow, Janvier."

"See you tomorrow, Chief."

Maigret wiped his brow before starting up the stairs. He was drenched in sweat.

"Someone called three times but wouldn't give me a number for you to call back. He'll try to get you again later."

"A man's voice? A woman's?"

"You couldn't tell. He or she kept saying that it was extremely important, a matter of life or death."

Just when Maigret, relaxed at last, was going to sit down for dinner in front of the open window. . . .

3

It was not until about nine o'clock that the sound of the telephone echoed through the apartment and Maigret rushed to it, turning off the television as he went.

"Hello. Is that Superintendent Maigret?"

He was hearing the famous voice at last.

"You don't know me, but I know you. I saw you again

this afternoon when you visited Line Marcia, and then when you went to the Sardine."

He had been told of a voice which could have been a man's or a woman's. As far as Maigret was concerned it was more that of a boy whose voice was breaking, and an expression which didn't mean anything came into his mind —a nutcracker voice. It continually shot from bass to treble and treble to bass.

"Who are you?"

"My name wouldn't mean anything to you. Inspector Louis doesn't know who I am either, and yet I've been calling him fairly frequently for years.

"I've tried to get hold of him today but he isn't at home or in his office. So I decided to speak directly to you. Tell me, when are you going to arrest him?"

"Whom?"

"You know as well as I do. Mori. Manuel Mori, for it's the elder one it's all about."

Maigret heard the noise of coins being put in. The unknown man was calling from a phone booth.

"It's urgent, Superintendent. It's a matter of life or death for me. You've put detectives on the tail of the two brothers. I saw them right away. The Moris are professionals and they'll certainly have seen them too. So they'll know that someone has talked, and *they* know me. They'll certainly think of me.

"I beg you, arrest Manuel at least. He's the more dangerous. He's the one who shot Monsieur Maurice."

"Why?"

There was suddenly silence at the other end of the line, and Maigret frowned. He waited for a long time, but the phone remained silent.

This time there was no chink of coins, but an emptiness. An agonizing emptiness.

"Did he tell you who he was?" Madame Maigret asked.

"No. He knows a lot and he's in danger."

He went to bed eventually, tired, worried. He had no way of protecting a man of whom he knew neither the identity nor the appearance.

When he got to the Quai des Orfèvres the following morning it was already hot, and he saw Inspector Louis waiting for him on one of the benches in the long corridor.

"Was it I you wanted to see?"

"Yes, Superintendent."

"Have you had any news from your kind informer?"

"Yes. He called me at night. He broke off his conversation with you because through the window of the booth he could see someone he didn't want to be seen by. He also told me that as long as the Mori brothers are at liberty he won't give any sign of life. He's going to go underground."

"Do you think he's really in danger?"

"Yes. If not, he wouldn't say he was."

"What rumors are circulating about Montmartre?"

"That it was all or nothing for one or the other of them, Manuel or Monsieur Maurice. They were both armed. I suppose Mori was the quicker on the draw."

"And the reason for the crime?"

"When I ask about it here and there, people just smile."

"Do you think Mori was Line Marcia's lover?"

"That had occurred to me. If it's true, she was risking not only her luck but probably her life."

"Have you been on Rue Ballu this morning?"

"There are already black draperies on the door and many people going in and out."

"Did you recognize any?"

"It's a mixture. Small shopkeepers, restaurant owners, night-club girls, pimps . . ."

"I'd like to have a look myself."

He called Janvier and asked him to have a car waiting in the yard.

"Come with me, Monsieur Louis. You know these people better than I do."

On Rue Ballu there were little groups gathered on the sidewalk as if it were the day of the funeral. The dramatic death of Monsieur Maurice was an event for all Montmartre, and people spoke of it in hushed voices.

"Let's go in."

They went up to the first floor. Silence reigned in the stairwell. The door of the apartment was ajar. From the hall one could smell the scent of candles and chrysanthemums. There were more flowers than there was room for them, and there was no need for greenery to make the vast living room appear less empty.

Line, standing near the door in full mourning, bowed her head to each visitor and shook hands with everyone who held out his hand to her. Her expression was fixed, impenetrable.

When she recognized Maigret her expression was one of annoyance, as if to reproach him for having come and for not respecting the dead.

"My sincere condolences," he stammered.

"I'm bearing up as best as I can."

The coffin was still open and Maurice could be seen, fully dressed, his face peaceful, with, it appeared, an ironic smile on his lips. The living room, hung in black with silver teardrops, was lit by a dozen candles whose scent spread throughout the entire place.

The visitors stopped for a moment to look at the body, which was ceremonially dressed.

"Do you recognize anyone?" whispered Maigret.

"A couple of pimps. The owner of the Sans-Gêne, with his wife, who runs the place with him . . ."

"Do you think this will go on all day?"

"Certainly. And the Church of Notre-Dame-de-Lorette will be too small to hold everyone."

They stopped a moment with others on the sidewalk opposite, watching the visitors go in and come out.

"Here they are."

A red Jaguar had just stopped at the corner of the street and two men, still very young, got out. They were both elegant, handsome boys, and there was a kind of defiance in their expression.

Everybody knew them, and they knew it. They walked down the middle of the street, bowing discreetly to right and left. When the elder brother saw Maigret he hesitated for a moment and then walked over to him.

"You're giving yourself a lot of trouble, Superintendent, having me and my brother followed. I can save you the expense of these tails by telling you what I'm going to be doing. This afternoon, for example, I'll be on Rue du Caire with Jo, because we have a big shipment coming in. Tomorrow, after the service, I'll be going to Bandol.

"As for you, Louis, you can go on ferreting about in corners and listening to gossip. Marcia deserved better than that."

Apparently satisfied with himself, he rejoined his brother and went into the house.

"There's an example for you of the kind of man he is," murmured Inspector Louis. "A young wolf with sharp fangs who thinks he's cleverer than anyone else."

"I'd like to talk to his concierge."

"She's on duty only in the daytime. At night it's her husband, who sleeps on a camp bed in the lodge. He's called Victor and he's well known in the neighborhood. He's an inveterate drunk who spends his days going from *bistrot* to *bistrot*."

53

"Could you get hold of him?"

"We'll try. We'll have to begin on Square La Bruyère and Place Saint-Georges."

In each of the *bistrots* Inspector Louis drank a quarter-bottle of Vichy. As for Maigret, he limited himself to a total of two glasses of beer.

"Have you seen Victor?"

"He was in here half an hour ago and he must have been just beginning his rounds, because he wasn't drunk yet."

When the two men caught up with him in the sixth *bistrot* he was starting to be seriously so.

"Good heavens, Inspector Louis! A quarter-bottle of Vichy for the inspector! And you, Fatso?"

He was a wreck, the type of man found under the bridges. His open shirt front exposed his chest, and one of his pockets was coming free from its seams.

"I bet you've come to see me. Who's this creep? A doctor?"

"Why would a doctor want to see you?"

"It wouldn't be the first time. They try to put me away, although I'm the most harmless character in the world."

That made him laugh.

"It's Superintendent Maigret."

"I've heard that name before. What does Superintendent Maigret want with me?"

"You sleep in the concierge's lodge at night, don't you?"

"Since my wife has been ill and the doctors have ordered her to rest."

"How many tenants are there in the house?"

"Oh, I've never counted them. Let's see, two apartments on each floor and an average of three people in each apartment. Count it up yourself. It's a long time since I've had anything to do with arithmetic."

"Do you know Manuel Mori well?"

"He's my friend."

"Why?"

"Because sometimes when he comes in he slips me a bottle. It never occurs to the others that I might be thirsty."

"Does he usually come in late?"

"That depends on what you mean by late. Give me that, Gaston."

The red wine dripped down his unshaven chin.

"Midnight?"

"What about midnight?"

"Did he come in about midnight?"

"Or about five in the morning. It depended on the night. When his girl came to see him . . ."

"You mean he brought women in?"

"No, monsieur. Not women. A woman."

"Always the same one, then?"

"Exactly, always the same one."

"Tall?"

"Not as tall as him, but taller than I am."

"Slim? Blonde?"

"And why wouldn't she be slim and blonde?"

"Did she spend the whole night with him?"

"Not at all. You haven't got the idea. She never stayed more than an hour or two."

"Do you know her name?"

"I'm not a policeman. What about you, do you know my name?"

"Victor."

"Victor what? Don't you think I have a surname like everybody else? Well, my name's Macoulet, like my father's and my mother's, and I was born near Arras. What do you say to that?"

"Was it when he came in with her that he slipped you a bottle?"

"Hey! That hadn't occurred to me. That might well be. That was the case the last time."

"When was the last time?"

"Yesterday? No. Day before yesterday. I get confused about time because all the days and all the nights are the same. It was the night the tenants on the first floor gave a party. The ceiling was shaking over my head and they didn't stop uncorking champagne bottles."

"What floor does Manuel Mori live on?"

"On the third. It's a beautiful apartment, believe you me. He didn't get the furniture in a junk shop or in a department store. For example, the bedroom is entirely hung in yellow silk. What do you say to that?"

"Did he come at the same time as she?"

"He always comes at the same time as she. I don't know if he's afraid someone will pinch her from him."

"Did nobody come in that night, when Mori and his girl friend were upstairs?"

"Let me think. Funny how thinking gives one a terrible thirst. Now, if you buy me a bottle . . ."

Maigret signaled the proprietor in his blue apron to serve him.

"Well, you know, I never see the people who go by. They ring at the front door without ever waking me completely. You mustn't tell that to the building manager, who's a rat. Right. I pull the cord, the people come in and say a name when they go by the glass door. That night the man, because he was by himself, said 'Mori.' I thought:

"'That's funny. He came in a minute ago with his girl.'

"But he might have gone out again to buy a bottle. Or maybe it wasn't him, but his brother. For there are two of them. Did you know there are two of them?

"He pressed the button of the stair light and he went up."

"By the stairs or by the elevator?"

"I wouldn't know about that. I went back to sleep."

"You didn't see him leave?"

"Leave, no. The door can be opened from the inside."

"Did no one make a noise going out?"

"God, yes! The crowd who were at the first floor. They were all stinking drunk, even the women yapping their way down the stairs."

"Did you get up and take a look at them?"

"No. I heard the door shut behind them and I didn't pay any more attention."

"And the girl friend?"

"What girl friend? You have one fault, Superintendent. You talk about everyone at the same time. Are you talking about the people on the first floor or about Mori?"

"About Manuel Mori and his mistress."

"Right. That's clearer already, although you've forgotten the brother."

"Did he go o t again alone?"

"The brother? I don't even know if it was the brother."

"Another beer," Maigret said. His forehead was covered with sweat. "All right. Let's say the visitor."

"I didn't hear him go out."

"And the floozy?"

"If you knew her, you wouldn't call her a floozy. She's a real lady."

"The lady, then?"

"She didn't stay up there more than half an hour."

"Did you see her go out?"

"No. Once again, no. If I had to get up to see people go out it wouldn't be worth having a bed."

"And after that Mori didn't come down with a heavy bundle?"

"My apologies. Didn't see a thing. No Mori, no bundle. But I heard the car start up."

"Mori's car?"

"Yes. A little red car, very powerful, which makes a lot of noise when it starts up."

"What time did he come back after that?"

"I don't know. But when he said his name as he went by I thought they were being excessive, on the third floor.

"If it hadn't been for the bottle . . ."

"There was a second bottle?"

"No. But the first one wasn't a common red like this. It was brandy."

"Thank you, Victor," Maigret called after paying the bill.

Once out in the street, the superintendent murmured:

"It seems that your informer . . ."

"What do you mean, my informer?"

"The one who calls you from time to time to give you tips."

"I never asked him to. I don't even know him."

"That's a pity, because he seems to be well informed. After what I've just heard, I'm beginning to believe that he's afraid. Do you think the Moris are capable of killing him?"

"Or of having him killed. I think they're capable of anything."

"I wonder if I shouldn't get a warrant from the magistrate to take them into custody."

"Both of them?"

"If the younger brother is as dangerous as Manuel . . ."

"What shall I do?"

"You go on picking up information in the neighborhood.

It's the right moment. People must be talking among themselves, exchanging information."

"Will you arrest them today?"

"I'm going to see them on Rue du Caire first."

Maigret went, however, to the magistrate's office. The
magistrate was a man of about fifty who had known Maigret
for a long time. His name was Bouteille.

"Are you bringing me the murderer this quickly?"

"Not quite. But I'm beginning to have a clearer picture
of the case."

Maigret told what he knew. The two men sat there face
to face, smoking their pipes.

When the superintendent had finished, the magistrate
growled:

"That's not much in the way of proof."

"I would like, when I go to see them, to have an order
for their arrest in my pocket. And also a search warrant."

"Made out in the name of both brothers?"

"That would be best. I don't know where the informer's
hide-out is. It would seem that Jo is as dangerous as
Manuel."

Judge Bouteille turned to his clerk.

"Make out two warrants in the names of the Mori
brothers, Manuel and Joseph."

Maigret gave the address of each one.

The magistrate led him to the door.

"The case is going to create a scandal."

"It's doing so already."

"I know. I've read the papers."

One of them set out its headline coldly:

"Was Maurice Marcia a Gang Leader and Was
He Killed by a Rival?"

Another made reference to all the little mysteries around Pigalle and to the role of the police force, which kept its eyes too often closed.

"The investigation looks as if it will be difficult and one wonders if we will ever know the end of the story.

"The funeral service tomorrow promises to attract a considerable crowd since the proprietor of the Sardine had friends not only in the neighborhood but all over Paris.

"It is true that they will not all be there.

"As for Superintendent Maigret, he refuses to make any statement. At the present moment it is not even known if he will go to Bandol tomorrow.

"He merely repeats:

" 'I am continuing with my investigation.' "

It was on the edge of Les Halles, where the buildings had not yet begun to be demolished, but where all activity had ceased and had been moved to Rungis.

Rue du Caire was one of the many streets where there were wholesalers and warehouses as well as hotels letting rooms by the hour, and shabby *bistrots.*

In a year's time everything would probably be a heap of rubble.

When Maigret got out of his taxi, he saw two detectives pacing the sidewalk. For a moment he wondered why there were two, then he understood. One was watching Manuel Mori and the other his brother Jo.

"You know they've spotted you, boys?"

"That's why we're not hiding. The elder one walked over to me quite calmly and said, blowing the smoke from his cigarette in my face, just like in the movies:

" 'Don't trouble to play hide-and-seek, copper. I know you're there and I won't try to get away '

The warehouse was a long, empty space without any step up from street level; at night, it would be shut by a sliding metal door. In the center of the space Maigret could see a truck unloading. One of the men, in a gray overall, was in the truck, passing down the boxes of fruit to his fellow workman, who caught them in mid-air and stacked them along the wall.

A few yards away, Jo Mori, his hands in his pockets, a cigarette in his mouth, was watching the unloading with the look of a man whose mind is on other things. He did not frown when he saw Maigret, did not make as if to move toward him.

In the right-hand corner of the warehouse, near the street, there was a glassed-in office where Manuel, hat on the back of his head, was going through a pile of receipts. He too had undoubtedly seen the superintendent, but he wasn't going to move.

Maigret pushed open the door, took the only empty chair and sat down, then began to fill his pipe.

It was Manuel who weakened first and murmured:

"I was expecting you."

Maigret still said nothing.

"Besides, I've just telephoned my lawyer. He agrees with me that you talk too much, you and that sad inspector who has been ferreting around Montmartre as long as anyone can remember. You're both asking too many people too many questions."

Maigret lit his pipe carefully without appearing to pay any attention to the man speaking to him.

"Sometimes insidious questions can do as much harm as accusations, and in that case it's slander.

"As far as my brother and I are concerned, it's all the same to us, but you're implicating other people. As for the

Flea, because he has stuck his nose into what is none of his business, it could be the end for him."

And so it was through one of the Mori brothers, without asking him anything, that Maigret finally learned the identity of the man who had telephoned him the previous evening and who phoned in information on a more or less regular basis to Inspector Louis.

"Where were you night before last at half past twelve?"

"At home."

"No. You had been there half an hour earlier and you weren't alone."

"I have the right to have any visitors I like."

"But not to murder people who come to visit you."

"I haven't murdered anyone."

"And I'm sure you don't have any gun, not even a .32 revolver."

"What would I do with one?"

"You found a use for one that night. It's true, you could always plead self-defense."

"I don't have to defend myself against anybody."

"I'd like to look over your apartment."

"Go and get a warrant from the magistrate."

Maigret took it out of his pocket and held it out to Manuel, together with the two warrants for arrest.

It was plain that Mori hadn't expected that, and he saw the danger, gave a start, and dropped cigarette ash over his vest.

"What does that mean?"

"What these papers usually mean."

"Are you going to haul me in?"

"I don't know yet. Probably. Do you still refuse to let me into your apartment?"

He got up for a moment, trying to recapture his arrogance. He opened the door slightly.

"Hey, Jo. Come here a minute."

His brother had taken off his jacket and rolled back the sleeves of his white shirt.

"You know what these papers mean, don't you? There's one for you, one for me, and another for the two of us, the search warrant. You haven't got a body stashed in your closet, have you?"

The younger Mori didn't join in the joking but read through the warrants carefully.

"Next move?" he asked.

One couldn't tell if he was speaking to his brother or to Maigret.

"When I've finished with your brother I'll go to your hotel. You wait for me there."

"Do you have a car?" asked Manuel.

"A taxi."

"You wouldn't rather I drove you?"

"No. But follow my taxi without trying to pass it."

Maigret picked up the detective charged with following Manuel.

"Where are we going?"

"To his place on Square La Bruyère."

"He's following us."

"That's just what I asked him to do."

It was only a stone's throw from Rue Fontaine. Marcia's apartment on Rue Ballu was a stone's throw from the restaurant. As for Jo, he lived in the Hôtel des Iles on Avenue Trudaine, only five minutes away.

"The funeral's tomorrow, but then the body's being taken to Bandol, where he'll be buried."

The six-floor building was modern, elegant.

"What shall I do? Shall I come up with you?"

"I'd rather you stayed downstairs."

The red Jaguar stopped behind the taxi.

"I'll show you the way."

They went past the lodge, where the curtain moved.

"It's on the third floor."

"I know."

"Doesn't it worry you, taking the elevator with me?"

"Not at all."

"You should be afraid. I'm younger and stronger than you."

Maigret merely looked at him as one looks at a boasting child.

Manuel took a key out of his pocket, opened the door, and ushered the superintendent in in front of him.

"You see, I have no maid. A woman comes in every day to do the cleaning, but as I'm often asleep at this time of day she only comes in the afternoons."

The sitting room was not big, particularly in comparison with the one on Rue Ballu, but it was furnished just as fastidiously. It led into a dining room where a still life by Chardin, showing pheasants in a basket, looked quite authentic to Maigret.

"Chardin?"

"I believe so."

"Do you like paintings?"

"I appreciate them quite a lot. The fact that I sell tomatoes and fruit doesn't mean I have no appreciation of the fine arts."

His tone was bantering. In the bedroom, the bed was unmade. This room was the only modern room, very bright, very gay. It gave onto a bathroom so big that there was a punchball set up in the middle.

"End of visit. You've seen everything."

"Not yet. There's something missing in the bedroom."

"What?"

"In the middle of the room there used to be a small rug which has left a lighter patch on the carpet."

Maigret leaned over.

"Besides, you can still see in the pile of this carpet colored threads that probably come from the missing rug."

"Look for it."

"I wouldn't be so stupid. May I?"

He picked up the telephone and asked for the Criminal Police, then for the laboratory.

"Is that you, Moers? This is Maigret. I want you to come to Square La Bruyère with two or three men. You'll find one of our detectives at the door. Go up to the third floor. What am I looking for? Anything."

This time Manuel had lost his arrogance.

"They'll come and turn over everything in the apartment."

"Very likely."

"I can tell you right now that the rug you're talking about has never existed."

"Then we'll find out what those colored threads came from."

"It's a girl friend's coat . . ."

"No. Madame Marcia—Line, if you prefer—is a woman of taste who wouldn't wear a coat mixing green with red and yellow."

"My lawyer has the right to be present during the search, I suppose?"

"As far as I'm concerned I've no objection."

It was Manuel's turn to make a phone call.

"Hello. May I speak to Maître Garcin, please. This is Manuel Mori. It's very urgent."

He was getting feverish.

"Garcin? Listen, I'm calling you from home. Superintendent Maigret has a search warrant. He has found some threads he doesn't like on the carpet. Suddenly he has called in men from the medico-legal department. Can you come?

"What's that? I am obliged to let them go through all the furniture and the drawers? That isn't all. He has a warrant for my brother's arrest and another in my name. . . .

"No. He told me that he doesn't know yet if he'll use them. Listen, if I haven't called you by, let's say, four this afternoon, do everything you can to get us out again. I have no wish to spend the night in the Mousetrap. Besides, the funeral service is tomorrow, and I was planning to go to Bandol afterward for the burial. . . .

"Yes, she's all right. Thanks, old man. See you later."

His conversation with the lawyer had bucked him up a bit.

He was surprised to hear Maigret say to him:

"If you had told me you were going to Bandol . . ."

"What difference would that have made?"

"I wouldn't have worried about the warrants just now. I wasn't thinking of Line, who will probably be needing you."

"What are you insinuating?"

"Only what everyone around Pigalle knows. You don't have two or three girl friends a week any more."

"My private life is my own business."

"You have the right to sleep with the wife of a friend, that's true, but not to shoot him in the chest."

The doorbell rang. Moers was accompanied by two men carrying small cases.

"This way. It's in the bedroom. No point in asking you what was on the paler patch . . ."

"A rug, of course."

"There are still some threads on the carpet. I'd like you

to collect them and study them. In general, the whole apartment needs a thorough going over. I would be interested to find plans of houses or châteaux, for example, or correspondence with antique dealers or art dealers.

This time Mori was dumfounded and made no attempt to hide it.

"What's all this about, this new angle?"

"It's nothing yet, just an idea, but it might turn into something.

"I'll let you get on with your work, Moers. I have something else to do. I may perhaps need you there too."

And, turning to Manuel:

"I'll leave you too. Until I give orders to the contrary, you are at liberty, but you are forbidden to leave the city."

"What about Bandol?"

"I'll tell you that tomorrow morning."

"May I telephone Line?"

"You've just come from there."

Manuel shrugged his shoulders.

"You've got so far it isn't worth denying it. Particularly since we have done nothing wrong."

"Congratulations."

Several minutes later Maigret entered the Hôtel des Iles, which, though not a luxury establishment, was comfortable and unusually clean, probably inhabited by permanent residents.

"Jo Mori, please."

The young lady on the other side of the counter looked at him, smiling.

"Second floor. Number 22, Monsieur Maigret."

"Did he tell you he was expecting me?"

"No. He told me he was expecting someone. But I recognized you as soon as you opened the door."

Maigret took the elevator, knocked at Number 22, and

the door opened at once. It was Jo, who had left Rue du Caire so that he would be at home when the superintendent arrived.

"What have you done with my brother?"

"I left him at home. With, it's true, specialists from the laboratory who are going over the place with a fine-tooth comb."

"You haven't arrested him?"

"Line will be needing him tomorrow. He has to go to Bandol. What about you?"

"I wasn't planning to go. What Line are you talking about?"

"You can let that drop. That's all finished with. Your brother has admitted he's her lover."

"I don't believe you."

They were in a little pearl-gray living room which was somewhat old-fashioned, but still pleasing. Jo, after hesitating, reached out for the phone and dialed his brother's number.

Maigret, his hands behind his back, looked around, opened a door at random, and found himself face to face with a girl who was wearing only a dressing gown that hung half open.

"You're Jo's mistress, I suppose? That's a stupid question, since I find you in his room, near the unmade bed, with some of your clothes on the chair."

"Is there anything wrong in that?"

"Not at all. How old are you?"

"Twenty-two."

He heard Jo's voice behind him.

"He's with her already. I didn't have time. What about you? Is it true he's letting you go to Bandol and that you've told him about Line? You might have warned me. . . .

"I don't know. He's talking with her in the bedroom now. You know her. She could talk for hours, but unfortunately I haven't found a deaf-mute who attracts me."

He hung up quickly and appeared framed in the doorway of the bedroom.

The girl was saying, "My name's Marcelle. Marcelle Vanier. I'm from Béziers, but I came to Paris as soon as I could."

"How long have you been with Jo?"

"A month, and I haven't any illusions about it. I don't think I'll last for another month."

"Pull your robe together," the young man said dryly.

And, turning to Maigret:

"If you were to tell me what you are looking for exactly, we might get somewhere. You know we have a truck being unloaded and then I have to deliver the stuff."

As if he hadn't heard, the superintendent went on speaking to Marcelle.

"Where were you night before last?"

"From what time?"

"From eleven o'clock."

"We had gone to the movies, Jo and I. We came back right after, because he was tired."

"At what time did the phone ring?"

She opened her mouth, shut it again, and looked questioningly at Mori.

"There's no harm in that," he said. "It was my brother, who was calling to tell me that he intended to make a trip to the provinces in the next few days."

"To Bandol?" the superintendent asked slyly.

"To Bandol or somewhere else. He didn't say."

"If he spoke of Bandol, it was a premonition, since Maurice Marcia wasn't dead then."

"What would I know about that?"

"It was in all the papers yesterday, with the time of death. About half an hour past midnight."

"That's quite possible and it doesn't interest me."

"Have you any paintings here?"

"What paintings?"

"I don't know. There are a lot of art lovers in this case."

"I'm not one."

"And this furniture is good, honest, hotel furniture."

"What else would it be?"

"Is this where you keep the receipts and the business papers?"

"On Rue du Caire, at the office, of course."

"Do you work, Mademoiselle Marcelle?"

"Not at the moment."

"What did you do before you met this fellow?"

"I was a barmaid in a bar on Rue de Ponthieu. Perhaps I made a mistake when I left my job."

"I'd agree with that."

"What do you advise me to do?"

"Watch out, you!" interrupted Jo, his fists clenched.

"Gently, boy. I'm not hauling you in today. Enjoy your freedom while it lasts. But don't take it into your head to leave Paris.

"Oh, yes! One more bit of advice: don't so much as touch the Flea, if you should come across him. That could cost you very dearly."

And Maigret went downstairs filling his pipe. He had forgotten the girl at the reception desk and he was surprised when a young voice called out to him:

"Good-by, Monsieur Maigret."

4

When he arrived at Quai des Orfèvres, Maigret called Janvier into his office immediately.

"Nothing new on the Marcia case?"

"Only a phone call from Inspector Louis, who would like to speak to you."

"Is he in his office?"

"No. He'll be in the Restaurant du Rhône, on Boulevard de Clichy, at half past twelve."

"Will you have lunch with me?"

"Yes. Besides, my wife is at her mother's today and I would have eaten in a restaurant anyway."

The superintendent called Madame Maigret.

"I'm very busy, and I won't be home for lunch."

She had known it in advance. Every time that a case got to a certain point he needed to play truant in a way, that is to say, to lunch with his colleagues at the Brasserie Dauphine.

It was a way of keeping his hand in.

The two men walked slowly over to the *brasserie* and stood at the counter, where there were already several men from Quai des Orfèvres.

"I'll have a small *pastis* for a change," growled Maigret.

That happened rarely. Since his old friend Pardon had warned him, he drank much less than before and he would keep his pipe in his mouth, unlighted, for a long time.

"You don't know what Louis wants with me?"

"Well, you know, he's always so mysterious."

"He's an amazing man, but he couldn't join our group. He needs to work alone."

The proprietor came over to shake hands with them. Little by little, he had grown completely bald and, as the process had taken years, it had gone unnoticed.

"What is for lunch?"

"*Andouillettes*. But if you would rather have a steak . . ."

"*Andouillettes*," Maigret cut in.

"Same for me," echoed Janvier.

They went into the dining room, where they found only four tables occupied, two of them by lawyers. They were among themselves, as it were; Maigret had his corner by the window from which he could see the Seine and the boats passing. From his office too he could see the boats going by, and that had been so for more than thirty years. But he never tired of it.

"When you get back to the Quai, would you please call the airport? I want a seat in a plane for Marseilles tomorrow. Preferably around noon."

"Are you going to Bandol?"

"Yes. Unofficially, of course, since it's out of our jurisdiction."

"There's certainly an Air-Inter flight."

"It's half past twelve. Would you call Inspector Louis and ask him to come to my office as soon as he has had lunch?"

By quarter past one the Widower was seated facing the superintendent, and the leaves on the trees rustled on the other side of the open window. Maigret had taken his jacket off. Louis was still in black, even his tie.

"I had a phone call this morning from the girl friend of my anonymous caller. . . ."

Maigret could not hide a smile.

"She didn't tell me her name. She's worried because her friend hasn't given any sign of life for forty-eight hours."

Maigret waited patiently for him to go on.

"Another rumor, more vague. At least three or four shady characters suddenly found the need to leave Montmartre. And, it just happens, they are friends of the Mori brothers."

"I have some news for you, too, Inspector. I know who your anonymous caller is."

Louis's face grew quite red. It seemed impossible to him that the superintendent could arrive in twenty-four hours at an identification which he had not been able to make over the years.

"Who is it?"

"Do you know the Flea?"

"Everyone in Montmartre knows him."

"It's he. Manuel Mori told me so himself, giving himself away or thinking that I knew already."

Maigret had known the man who was called the Flea, because he was only four feet eleven, for almost thirty years. He was also thin, with a strange face in which the mouth took up almost all the space. And that mouth could take on every possible expression in an instant, as if it were made of rubber.

He had worked as a messenger boy at the Cellar Rat, a cabaret on Place Pigalle which was then very elegant, where most of the customers wore dinner jackets. He wore a red uniform with a short jacket, a braided cap, and he stood at the door, ready to take customers' messages anywhere.

The Cellar Rat had disappeared. The Flea, whose real name was Justin Crotton, had worked for several years in the *brasserie* on Rue Victor Massé where the underworld gang bosses hung out.

He was still just as thin, just as agile, as capable of slipping in anywhere, but his face was lined. From a distance he looked like a boy. Close up, he fully looked his age of forty-five or forty-six.

"And to think I didn't recognize his voice," Louis moaned.

"He must have disguised it as much as possible."

"Not so much as all that. Now that you've told me, I can see it. I can't forgive myself for not having thought of him."

"What has he been doing lately?"

"He had shacked up with a hostess at the Canary on Rue Pigalle, who lives on Rue Fromentin."

"Her pimp?"

"More or less. I don't know. It's a bit strange for a pretty girl to set up house with a runt like that. He was born in Paris, on Boulevard de la Chapelle, and I needn't tell you what his mother did for a living. She sent him to one of her sisters at Saint-Mesmin-le-Vieux, in the Vendée. He came back to Paris when he was fourteen and managed to get by on his own."

"He's in danger," Maigret said gravely.

"Do you think the Moris would dare . . . ?"

"They themselves are out of it. But they have enough killers at their disposal to eliminate a troublesome witness."

Inspector Louis couldn't keep off the subject.

"The Flea! And nobody suspected him. He was considered an inoffensive creature, not quite a man, a kind of boy with a wrinkled face. He hung around rogues who wouldn't be embarrassed by talking in front of him.

"I think he dreamed of being one of them. I wouldn't be surprised if they hadn't used him for a lookout from time to time."

"What's the name of his girl friend?"

"Blanche Pigoud. 28 Rue Fromentin. A stone's throw from Boulevard de Clichy, where I've just been having lunch."

"Do you know her?"

"Only by sight. I've never had anything on her."

"She must go to bed in the small hours. We're likely to find her at home."

"Unless it's her day at the hairdresser's. Those girls only get up early to go to the hairdresser."

Maigret called Janvier.

"Do you want to come with us? We're going to Montmartre again."

"Shall I take a car?"

"Of course."

The three of them went off. It was a beautiful day, a little too warm for May, and it felt as if there might be a thunderstorm.

Rue Fromentin was quiet. Number 28 was a fairly modern, well-built apartment block.

"Shall we all go up?"

"I'll go up alone first, so as not to frighten her. No, wait. It would be better if Inspector Louis came with me, since he's the one she phoned."

"Second floor on the street," the concierge told them.

Kitchen smells hung around the stairwell, and a baby was crying somewhere. Maigret rang the bell. It was a long time before a young, rather plump girl, naked under a light robe, opened the door.

She recognized Inspector Louis.

"Have you found him?"

"Not yet, but Superintendent Maigret would like to talk to you."

"Just look at me! I was asleep. I haven't even combed my hair."

"We'll give you time for that," Maigret said jovially.

The girl had an open expression, even a little naïve. She must have been about twenty-five, and life had not yet taken away all her freshness.

"Come in. Sit down. I'll be with you right away."

She went into a bedroom which must have opened onto the bathroom.

If the superintendent had not been used to some women of the kind scorned by middle-class ladies, he would have been surprised by the décor surrounding them.

The living room was comfortably furnished. The same

so-called modern furniture could be found in half the apartments in Paris. The wood was carefully waxed, as was the
floor. Besides which, there was a slight smell of disinfectant
everywhere.

Pushing open a door, Maigret discovered an immaculate
kitchen where not a thing was out of place.

"Would you like a cup of coffee?" asked the girl when
she reappeared, still naked under her robe, but with her
face washed and a light coating of make-up on.

"No, thank you."

"Do you mind if I have one? In my job, I can't always
refuse a drink. When he can, Bob serves me cold tea to
look like whiskey, but with some customers that's not possible. If you'd like, there's beer in the icebox. Justin adores
beer and he's always hoping it will make him get fat. Did
you know he weighs only ninety pounds?"

"He was going to be a jockey, but his training lasted only
two days because he was afraid of the horses."

"He isn't afraid of the Pigalle toughs."

She had switched on an electric percolator. The kitchen
was fitted out with all the most modern gadgets.

"You didn't say, about the beer."

"I would like a glass."

"Your inspector drinks only Vichy, and I haven't got
any."

"How do you know he drinks only Vichy?"

"He comes into the Canary from time to time. He goes
into all the *boîtes*. He sits at a corner of the bar and listens.
He knows a lot more than he looks as if he knows."

"Did you know about the Flea's telephone calls?"

"Not exactly."

She took her coffee into the living room, and Maigret
followed her with his glass of beer.

"He's a funny boy. Inspector Louis can tell you that, can't you, Inspector?"

"I've always wondered why you've set up house with him."

"First of all, because I can't stand most pimps. Really I was born to be a good little middle-class housewife and I'm never as happy as when I'm doing housework."

They were all sitting in armchairs.

"But in my job one needs a man."

"Even if he's a little runt like Justin Crotton?"

"Don't you believe that. He has stayed a child in certain ways, but he has more to him than he lets on."

She paid no attention to the robe which was hanging wide open. Her skin was very pale, probably very soft.

"His dream has always been to become one of the real toughs. To start off, like most of them, he wanted to be a pimp."

"Is that what he is now?"

"That's what I let him think. That lets him take himself seriously. He still runs messages for people as he did when he was a messenger boy. From time to time he puts on mysterious airs, even with me, and he just says:

" 'Don't be surprised if I don't come for a night or two. We have something big on.' "

"Was it true?"

"It was true that something big was being prepared by one gang or another but he wasn't in it. What I didn't know was that he would phone all the information he had to the inspector. That also made him feel more important in his own eyes."

"What has been happening these last two days? Has he told you?"

"Not exactly. One morning he came in overexcited.

" 'There was a row last night, something that will be on the front page of all the papers, and there'll be a great scandal.'

" 'A robbery?'

" 'Worse than that. A murder. And the victim is one of the best-known people in the neighborhood.'

" 'Can't you tell me his name?'

" 'It'll be in all the papers soon. It's Monsieur Maurice.'

" 'The proprietor of the Sardine?'

" 'Yes. And I'm the only person, besides the murderer and his mistress, who knows who did it.'

" 'I'd rather not know who it is.' "

She lit another cigarette, for she had already lit one when she came out of the bathroom.

"I asked him what he was going to do. He answered:

" 'Don't worry about me.'

" 'You're not going to inform on the man, are you?'

" 'You know that's not my line.'

" 'Does the man know you know?'

" 'If he knew, I wouldn't make old bones.' "

She was silent for a moment, blowing the smoke in front of her.

"In a way it was the biggest day of his life.

" 'If you knew what it was all about . . . One of the biggest bosses of Montmartre . . . As for his mistress . . .'

" 'Don't tell me anything.'

" 'All right. You'll learn the truth in the papers. If the papers dare to publish it.'

"He went out that morning, and I haven't seen him since. Last night at the Canary people were looking at me in a funny way, and two men I don't know never took their eyes off me.

"I stayed at the bar as usual. I was joined by a customer

from the provinces who always comes to see me when he's in Paris. We went to the hotel and when we came out one of the men was walking up and down on the sidewalk.

"At first I was afraid for the Flea. Everyone calls him that, and now I do too. Besides, he's quite proud of it. It's a kind of recognition. He likes to make faces too, to amuse people."

"He called me," said Inspector Louis in a neutral voice.

"That's what I thought. That explains his mysterious manner, and what he said when he went. Is he really in danger?"

It was Maigret who answered.

"There's no doubt about that. Monsieur Maurice's murderer knows that the Flea has informed on him."

"What about me? Do you think they will get at me?"

"Are you still being followed?"

"Last night one of the men was still at the Canary. He was called to the telephone and he went away after that, not without giving me a funny look."

"If I'm not mistaken, they're running to ground all over France."

"What about the Mori brothers?"

"Who told you about them?"

For there had been no mention of them in the papers or on the radio.

"Everyone around here is talking about them. Have they gone too?"

"No. But we're keeping an eye on both of them."

"Do you think it was they?"

"I can't answer that question. What time do you usually leave the house?"

"I do my marketing at about two or three, because I like to cook. At about ten in the evening I get dressed for work and I go to the Canary. I sit at the bar and I wait. Sometimes I wait for two hours or so, sometimes only a few minutes, and I have been known to wait until closing time."

"In an hour there'll be a plain-clothes policeman in the street. Don't be surprised when he follows you. He'll do everything he can, and more, to protect you."

"Should I go to the funeral service tomorrow? Everyone's going."

"Yes, do. I'll be there too. Just like your guardian angel."

"That makes me think of my catechism."

The two men stood up.

"If you hear anything, call the Criminal Police. Ask to speak to me, or to one of my men in the Criminal Division. Inspector Louis is rarely in his office."

"Thank you, Superintendent. Good-by, Inspector! If you have any news of Justin . . ."

"I hope we won't have any. He has recognized danger and has gone into hiding. He doesn't need to go far, for he knows Montmartre inside out and there are places where a boy like him can live for weeks without being seen."

"Let's hope so," she said, touching the wooden table.

They found Janvier outside.

"Well?"

"She's afraid, of course, and I can't blame her. Afraid for the Flea and for herself. I promised her that one of our men would be in front of the house in an hour and that she would be followed wherever she went. Don't forget to arrange it when we get back to the Quai. Someone who can go into a fairly elegant boîte without being conspicuous."

Maigret turned back to Louis.

"You stay on watch for the present. As soon as our man gets here you'll be free again."

"Right, Superintendent."

Once he was at the wheel again, Janvier asked:

"What's she like?"

"Very nice. If things had gone differently for her, probably when she was about seventeen or eighteen, she would have been a marvelous wife and housekeeper."

"Did she know anything?"

"About the Flea's phone calls? She only suspected it two days ago. It's extraordinary. That little man with the clown's face has been able to be one of Inspector Louis's informers for years without anyone suspecting. He must have enjoyed that role which gave him confidence in himself. When this man or that was arrested he could say to himself:

" 'That was my doing.'

"And it was true!"

During the afternoon Maigret went up to the attics of the Law Courts Building, where Moers's empire was: the forensic laboratory.

Specialists were needed in nine out of ten cases, even if only for fingerprints, and yet there were fewer than a dozen of them in white overalls working in the rooms with sloping ceilings.

"I suppose it's too soon to have any news?"

Moers was an unassuming man, thin as a rail, whose suit always needed pressing. He had been at the Quai for so long that it was impossible to imagine Criminal Records without him. He was always ready for work, whatever the hour of day or night. True, he was a bachelor and there was no one waiting for him in his student's lodgings in the Latin Quarter.

"One fact is already clear," he answered in his rather monotonous voice. "Quite recently, yesterday afternoon, probably, all the furniture has been polished, all the door-knobs wiped, the ashtrays, even the smallest object, to remove fingerprints.

"The only prints we lifted were those of the tenant, Manuel Mori, whose card I found in Records, and those of the cleaning woman, who did go to Square La Bruyère yesterday afternoon, the concierge told me. I forgot some other prints—yours."

"Not one fingerprint overlooked?"

"Not one. One would almost say professional work."

"It is professional work. What is the date of the card you found in Records?"

"It's fourteen years old."

"Theft?"

"Yes, during the vacation period, in a private house on Avenue Hoche."

"How many years did he get?"

"He was only eighteen, and it was his first offense. Besides, he was considered to be only an accomplice, since five men were involved."

"That reminds me vaguely of something, but I didn't have anything to do with the case personally."

"He got off with one year."

"Is there the slightest indication that a woman might have come regularly to the apartment, including the bedroom?"

"The closets and drawers have been gone over with a fine-tooth comb. Not a trace of face powder anywhere, no cream, not even a woman's hair."

"What about the carpet?"

"Dorin is without doubt one of the best authorities in the world on animal or vegetable fibers. He's nuts about them.

He spent more than an hour studying the carpet with a magnifying glass and he collected about thirty barely visible threads. He has been working on them for hours. When I say threads, I mean silk threads. They are very old, at least three hundred years, and Dorin would swear they come from a Chinese rug.

"He's still analyzing his find, because he wants to be absolutely accurate."

Maigret liked the atmosphere of these attic rooms, where the men worked quietly, away from the public gaze.

Each man knew what he had to do. The articulated dummy that was used so often in reconstructions stood near one of the gable windows. It was used to discover, for example, in what position a man would be found if he had been struck by a knife in such a way, or if a bullet had followed a particular trajectory.

"If there's anything new tomorrow, tell Janvier. I'll be in Bandol."

Moers was not the kind of man to take his holidays on the Riviera, and for him Bandol must have been like something in a dream.

"You'll be hot," was all he murmured.

When Maigret announced to his wife at dinner that he was going to Bandol the next day, she smiled and said:

"I knew that already."

"How?"

"Because the radio said just a moment ago that although the service would be in the Church of Notre-Dame-de-Lorette tomorrow morning, the actual burial would be in the Bandol cemetery. What do you expect to find out there?"

"Nothing definite. Perhaps a hint, just something. I'm going there for the same reason that I'm going to the service tomorrow."

"You'll be hot."

"I may have to spend the night there. That depends on planes. I can't bring myself to come back to Paris by train."

"I'll pack your blue overnight bag."

"Thank you. Just shirts and my toilet bag."

He felt a little guilty at going to the Midi at the taxpayers' expense, because it was not necessary. There was even a chance that he would discover nothing at all.

He slept well, as he almost always did, and was blinded by the sunlight when Madame Maigret brought him his first cup of coffee.

"They say it'll be ninety degrees in Marseilles today," she said, smiling.

"What about Paris?"

"Eighty-six. The hottest May in thirty-two years."

"My plane is at twelve something, I'm not sure exactly what, because Janvier saw to the ticket. I'll have just enough time to look in at the Quai before going to Orly. I'll take my bag now."

"What about your lunch? Where and when will you have it?"

"I'll have a sandwich at the bar at Orly."

He was going toward the door when she said:

"Aren't you going to give me a kiss?"

He would have come back to do so anyway.

"Don't be worried. I'm not taking a fifty-year-old, single-engine plane, and I'm not going around the world."

He felt a little emotional just the same, as he did each time he left his wife for more than a day.

Once out on the sidewalk he raised his head, and he knew in advance that he would see her looking out the window.

It was just as well that he did, for she was holding up the blue bag which he had forgotten, and they met halfway up the stairs.

It was quarter past nine when Janvier went into the superintendent's office.

"It seems the street is already full and that the church won't be able to hold everyone."

Maigret had been expecting something of the kind, but not quite to that point.

"Still no news of the Flea?"

"No. Blanche Pigoud had a phone call at the Canary last night. When she took her seat at the bar again she seemed excited, but almost immediately afterward a customer came and sat with her."

"What time did she go home?"

"About four in the morning."

"Too bad," Maigret growled to himself.

And he looked up the girl's number, found it, and called. Contrary to his expectations, it was not long before she answered.

"Who is it?" she asked in a sleepy voice.

"Superintendent Maigret."

"Have you any news?"

"No. You do. Who telephoned you last night at the Canary?"

"You're right. It was he."

"Did he tell you where he was?"

"No. He wanted to know if you or Inspector Louis were up to date on things concerning him. I said yes. Then he asked me if you were angry, and that time I said no."

She sounded like a child swollen with sleep.

"It's true, isn't it? You aren't angry with him?"

"Is he still as afraid?"

"Yes. He wanted to know, too, if there were any strangers hanging around the house.

" 'Hasn't anyone been arrested yet?'

" 'Not as far as I know.'

" 'They haven't searched Manuel Mori's place?'

" 'I think they have. The superintendent came here with Inspector Louis, but they didn't give me any details. In any case, there's a policeman watching over me day and night.' "

"He didn't say anything else?" asked Maigret.

"Only that he was changing his place every night. That's all. I didn't have time to say much to him, because a customer had been hanging around me for some time."

"Go back to bed and don't be afraid of anything. If you have anything new to tell me during the day, call Inspector Janvier at Quai des Orfèvres."

"Are you going to Bandol?"

He was beginning to be irritated by it. Everyone talked to him about this trip as if he had announced it in the papers.

"There you are!" he sighed, looking at Janvier, whose body was silhouetted against the green of the trees. "I don't know if it's a good idea, but he's changing his hiding place every night."

"Perhaps it's just as well. There must be so many people looking for him. . . ."

If, as was probable, Mori had given the word, all the crooks of Montmartre must be looking for the Flea. And he, with his build, could hardly pass unnoticed in a crowd.

"I'll come back shortly to pick up my bag. You'd better give me my plane ticket now."

Luckily, the departure time was later than he had feared —12:55.

"See you soon."

He had himself driven to Rue Ballu and told the policeman who was driving him to wait for him near the church.

More than two hundred people were crowded in front of the house, but only a few went in to present their condolences. There were people of all sorts, local shopkeepers, pimps, restaurant or night-club proprietors.

They began to bring the flowers down, and it took two cars to hold them and the wreaths.

Then four men brought down the mahogany coffin, which they slid into the hearse.

The church was quite near, and there wouldn't have been enough cars for everyone. When Line Marcia appeared on the doorstep in full mourning, blonde and pale, there was a movement in the crowd, as if a film star had passed by, and it seemed for a moment as if people were going to applaud.

She took her place in a huge black car which moved along at walking pace. All the personnel of the Sardine walked in front. They were followed by a group of elderly men, men of Monsieur Maurice's age, and some even older.

Very dignified, they walked along bareheaded, while the curious came to the windows to look.

Under a triumphant sun, the procession did not lack style, and Marcia would have been pleased with such a funeral.

When Maigret turned round, he saw that the procession extended over more than three hundred yards and the traffic had been rerouted by policemen who were making feverish gestures with white batons.

"A fantastic funeral!" cried a boy who was passing.

It was true that the church was already full except for the first rows, which had been cordoned off from the others with black ropes.

Line walked alone, still at the front, very straight, her blue eyes impenetrable.

She sat alone in the first row, while the employees sat in

the second. There were people standing in the two naves. Outside there were more, and the great doors had been left open, so that one felt the spring breezes.

The organ played a funeral march and a few moments later the service began.

Maigret, standing in the left aisle, was looking at faces, and it was not long before he saw Mori's. He had taken his place in the row of important people, people of authority, as if it was his by right, although he was the youngest.

His look met Maigret's and he showed a sort of defiance.

The superintendent didn't wait until the end of the service. He was hot. He was thirsty. A few minutes later he plunged into the shade of a *bistrot*, where he asked for a glass of beer.

"As funerals go, it's a fine funeral," growled the proprietor, who was very old and whose hand trembled a little. "Who is it?"

"The proprietor of the Sardine."

"At the head of Rue Fontaine?"

"Yes."

"I thought it was a gangster."

"He was, in his younger days."

Maigret drank his beer in one swallow, paid, and went to find the black police car.

"Take me to the Quai."

"Right, Chief."

It was eleven o'clock, just time to pick up his bag and shake Janvier's hand. Then Maigret went to Orly in the same car.

Were Line and Manuel going to travel together? Would the coffin be taken to Bandol by plane?

After the formalities had been gone through, he still had a little time and he went to look for the manager of the airport. It was a man he knew; he had worked at Quai des Orfèvres.

"Are you going to Bandol?"

Maigret had to control his anger.

"Yes. I think I leave in about twenty minutes."

"They'll be calling the passengers very soon."

"Tell me, do you know if a plane has been chartered to carry a coffin?"

"Monsieur Maurice's?"

"Yes."

"He'll go with his wife aboard a private plane which she has rented, he in the box, she outside, of course."

Maigret decided not to shrug his shoulders.

"How long will it take them to make the trip?"

"They're to land at Toulon. From there a hearse will take the coffin to Bandol. It's only ten miles."

"Passengers for Marseilles," the loud-speaker began.

And Maigret went to the gate that was pointed out to him. Ten minutes later the plane, a twin-engine machine, took off.

He had promised himself to took at the scenery, because he was especially fond of the countryside south of Lyons. He didn't have the chance, because he was asleep long before they flew over the Rhône.

From the airport at Marseilles he was taken to the station, and there was a train for Bandol half an hour later.

He felt a little ridiculous with his bag on his knees and his hat which he kept removing to wipe his forehead.

At Bandol, right from the station platform, the sun literally burned his skin and he began to regret having come. Taxis were waiting, as was a horse-drawn carriage, and Maigret chose the carriage.

"Where'll I take you, boss?"

"Do you know a decent hotel near the sea?"

"I'll have you there in fifteen minutes."

The wheels sank slightly into the asphalt softened by the heat. The town was almost white, like Algiers, and there were palm trees along some avenues.

He saw the sea, flag blue, through the greenery. Then he saw the beach where only a few people were sun-bathing while half a dozen swimmers were in the water. The season had not yet begun.

They had passed the Casino. The hotel was white too, with an enormous terrace sprinkled with colored parasols.

"Have you a room?"

"For how long?"

"Just for one night."

"A single? Would you like a sea view?"

He filled out the hotel questionnaire.

"Room number 233."

The hotel was called The Tamarisks. It was cool and very clean.

"Where can I get something to drink?"

"The bar is in there on the right."

He went in and drank a glass of beer.

"Aren't you Superintendent Maigret?" the bartender asked him after looking at him for a moment.

He was a young man, very blond, and blushed at his own daring.

"Are you here for a long time?"

"Just till tomorrow."

"I thought so. You've come for Monsieur Maurice's burial, haven't you?"

"Was he well known around here?"

"You might as well say he was God Himself."

"Is his villa far from here?"

"About a fifteen-minute walk. It's almost at the other end of the quay, not far from the villa of the late Raimu. You'll recognize it because there's an enormous swimming pool."

Maigret still had the impression of cheating, of taking an unauthorized holiday.

"And the cemetery?"

"Less than a mile from the villa. There's going to be quite a crowd there, you know. They've been arriving from Toulon and Marseilles since this morning."

"What kind of people?"

"Important people. I even wonder if the assistant commissioner won't come. Some people say he will."

Maigret downed a second beer and, after consulting his watch, started to walk. Fortunately, the avenues along the quay were shady.

The plane must have unloaded the coffin, and Line, at Toulon. The farther he walked, the more people he saw, and when he turned a corner there was almost the same sight as that morning on Rue Ballu.

How many of those people knew the truth? It didn't matter, for none of them would tell it.

Only one person had done so, from a public phone booth, without giving his name, and he had gone underground heaven knew where in Montmartre.

5

Slightly apart from the crowd he saw a face he knew well. It was Boutang, Superintendent of the Criminal Police in Toulon.

"It's funny," Boutang said, shaking him by the hand. "I thought of you this morning when I was shaving, and I had the feeling that you would come."

He pointed to the crowd.

"What do you think of that? What a haul we could make. Not only are the cream of all the gangsters of Toulon there, but also those of Marseilles, Cannes, Nice. . . ."

Someone came up to them and Boutang shook his hand, introducing the men to each other.

"Charmeroy, Superintendent of Police in Bandol. I suppose you recognized Superintendent Maigret, Charmeroy?"

"Glad to meet you."

They were both big men. Professionals who knew their job and weren't easily intimidated.

"Nine tenths of these people you see here live on the edge of the law, and the extraordinary thing is that there isn't one against whom we have any proof."

"When Marcia lived in Bandol in the summer, did he have many guests?"

"No, very few. A few close friends. The Mori brothers in particular."

"Did they sleep at the villa?"

"Yes. And, as it happened, it was always at the time of the big burglaries. You must have read about them in the papers. Summer residents who have a big villa on the coast, who have a yacht too and take a cruise to the Greek islands in July or August—when they get back they are very surprised not to find their furniture and their valuables."

"Just like the châteaux."

"Almost. I suspected the Mori brothers and even the big man, whom everyone around here calls Monsieur Maurice. I had the villa watched. As if by chance, every time there was a robbery the Moris didn't leave the villa and were playing gin rummy with Marcia into the small hours. Do you know his wife? She has a bit of class and seems out of place in that atmosphere."

The funeral procession arrived. Behind the hearse Line

sat alone in a car. Then other cars with Riviera license plates followed: big American cars, but also fast sports cars with the younger set.

They all moved at a walking pace and there was another crowd that followed as best it could.

There was a moment of confusion. The driver of the hearse was on the point of turning to the right when he drew near to the villa, but the master of ceremonies rushed up to give him other instructions.

The two groups mingled. It seemed as if everyone knew everyone else. They shook hands. Some spoke in whispers.

Madame Marcia got out of the car and went to the villa. She had changed since the morning. She was now wearing a black suit of a light material and a white silk hat. Her gloves were white too.

What had she come to do, alone, in the villa? Maigret could find no plausible answer to that question. Nor could Boutang or the local superintendent.

She stayed away less than ten minutes and got back into the car. The procession made a half turn, went into Rue des Ecoles, then Avenue du 11 Novembre, where they found themselves suddenly at the gates of the cemetery.

Confusion reigned again, for many people ran across the graves to get a good place near the open trench.

A priest was there and greeted Line.

She was not weeping, any more than she had wept in the morning at the Church of Notre-Dame-de-Lorette. The heavy coffin was lowered. The priest mumbled a few prayers; then the flowers that had been heaped on the neighboring tombs were put on the grave.

"All the top gangsters are there. The young ones too, proud to be seen with them. What are you going to do now, Superintendent?"

"I don't know."

"Where are you staying?"

"At The Tamarisks."

"It's very good and the owners are nice people."

Line had already driven off to the villa. Maigret, in the crowd, hadn't seen Manuel Mori or his brother.

"I think I'm going to make a visit."

"Do you think she was in on things?"

"I don't think, I'm certain. Unfortunately, I have no proof."

"Good luck. If you need me, you know where to find me, and where to find Charmeroy."

The crowd dispersed little by little and went to the center of town to slake its thirst in the bars. Only a few cars, those of the more important people, went directly to Toulon or Marseilles.

Maigret found himself alone in front of the white villa. It was not of an enormous size. It was a pretty villa, nothing more, and the most striking thing about it was the swimming pool surrounded by deck chairs. The garden was composed of a few palm trees, many cacti, and more or less tropical plants which Maigret was not familiar with.

He took the steps in three strides, rang the electric bell, and was surprised to see the door open immediately and Line standing in front of him.

"I might have guessed that you wouldn't miss the chance. You have no respect for mourning, have you?"

"What about you?"

They went straight into a huge hall with white walls where the furniture and furnishings were as excellent, in a different style, as those in the old house on Rue Ballu.

She did not ask him to sit down. She waited, standing, for him to start the conversation. The hand holding her cigarette trembled a little.

"I want to talk to you about the night your husband died."

"I thought I had already answered you on that subject."

"Since you didn't tell the truth, I shall ask you the question again."

And Maigret sat down in one of the cream-colored leather armchairs.

"You're taking advantage of the fact that I'm not strong enough to throw you out."

"You wouldn't dare do that anyway. If only so as not to implicate your lover."

She turned pale with rage and stubbed out her cigarette in an ashtray.

"Have you no humanity?"

"I have more than enough, in fact. But that depends on whom I am talking to. You obviously married Marcia for his money."

"That's my business."

She sat down at last, crossed her legs, lit a new cigarette which she took out of a gold box lying on the table.

"You were in bed, you and Manuel. Someone knocked loudly at the door and I imagine Mori put on a dressing gown while you wrapped yourself in the sheets."

She didn't turn a hair. The face was impassive now. One might even have sworn that there was nothing but curiosity in her pale blue eyes.

"And then?"

"It was your husband."

"And what did he do, do you think? Did he shake hands with Manuel?"

"He took his gun out of his pocket."

"Just like a movie . . ."

"What I want to know is where Mori's gun was. In some

piece of furniture, certainly. But it could as easily have been in the bedroom as in the living room."

"You must first prove that there was a gun in the apartment."

She lit her cigarette.

"And that I was there. And that there was a visitor who was none other than my husband. You've started badly, Superintendent."

Maigret was going to answer when she spoke in a voice hardly any louder.

"Come in, dear."

And immediately a door opened and Manuel appeared in shorts and espadrilles, as if he had come from the beach. "Well, Superintendent, you do get around, don't you?"

His gaze ran insolently over Maigret from head to foot; then he went to the bar and made himself a Tom Collins.

"Do you want one too, my dear?"

"I am thirsty."

"What about you, copper?"

"No."

"As you like. It's useless for you to show me your little yellow paper here. You're well out of your territory."

"I could get a warrant to take evidence without any difficulty."

"But you won't."

"Why not?"

"Because you have nothing against me."

"Not even the Flea's evidence?"

"Have you found him?" Manuel frowned.

"The Flea is without doubt the man, if you can call him that, who knows the 9th and 18th *arrondissements* best. The people know him too, and most of them are ready to put their hands on him. You won't be the one to find him,

Superintendent. My men will. But you won't have any proof of that, either. You see, I'm putting my cards on the table.

"If we had witnesses here, I would swear once more that I didn't shoot, that no shot was fired in my apartment, and that Maurice didn't set foot there that night.

"We would repeat too, Line and I, that there had never been anything between us, and I defy you to produce people who would say the contrary in court."

He was not acting. He was swollen with pride and Maigret wondered unhappily at the reason for his assurance. He seemed to fear nothing now, and Line was as calm as if a man called Marcia had never existed.

The superintendent thought suddenly of the Flea. Had Mori's men, as he called them, finally got their hands on the midget? Had they fixed him so that he would not be dangerous any more and so that he would keep quiet once and for all?

Maigret filled his pipe, lit it, stood up, and began to walk about the room.

"I am in fact out of my jurisdiction. I can't use the documents I showed you in Paris. . . ."

"Exactly."

"It would only need a phone call for Superintendent Boutang to be here in half an hour with a search warrant. I suppose you know Boutang?"

"He's no friend of mine."

"Well, it's up to you. Either you allow me to look through the villa or I call Toulon."

"Look it over, do. As long as you don't take anything away."

In the big living room itself, the superintendent made a discovery. One of the walls was covered with a bookcase in which all the books, as in Paris, were richly bound.

On the lower shelves there were piles of magazines. Not weeklies such as are found at any newsstand, nor did they fit with Monsieur Maurice's character. Maigret read out the titles in a low voice, checking to see whether the magazines had at least been leafed through.

"*Farms and Castles* . . . Very interesting reading, isn't it? *Country Life . . . The Connoisseur.*"

Mori frowned and glanced at his mistress.

"They're mine," she said. "I don't play cards, and when the men play gin rummy, I sit in a corner and read."

The next room was a dining room in antique Provençal style, and to the left was a boudoir in which every piece of furniture, as in Paris, was a museum piece.

"Is it genuine?" Maigret asked, pointing to a Van Gogh. It was the woman who answered.

"I'm not an expert, but my husband didn't usually buy fakes."

The kitchen was vast, modern, spotless.

"And yet you had few guests."

"How do you know?"

"I've had time to get information. I also know that the Mori brothers spent about a month a year with you."

"They were my husband's best friends."

"He probably didn't know anything about your relationship with Manuel."

Manuel still hadn't turned a hair and was listening to Maigret without saying a word.

"You're wrong. My husband was sixty-two and had had a good life. In one sense he was worn out. He was perhaps in love with me when he married me five years ago, but it wasn't long before we began to live like brother and sister."

"You can go on lying. It doesn't upset me."

He climbed a marble staircase and pushed open a double

door that opened into a vast bedroom which ended in a terrace overlooking the sea.

"Your room?"

There were twin beds, and more remarkably fine furniture.

The bathroom was even bigger than the one on Rue Ballu, and completely lined in yellow marble.

"Just one bathroom for the two of you. That doesn't fit in with your story of brother and sister."

"You can think what you like."

There were two other bedrooms upstairs, each with its bathroom.

"The Mori brothers, I suppose."

"Guest rooms."

"Apart from them, were there many other guests to use these rooms?"

"It happened."

The pictures were almost all old paintings by painters Maigret didn't know.

"Is there an attic?"

"Just the mansard attic where the servants sleep."

"Are they here now?"

"No. I'm leaving tonight. A cleaning woman is all that is needed to keep the villa in order."

"And you inevitably engage a different staff each year."

"We do change, yes."

"So that for most of the year this house is empty at night and there is no one to keep an eye on it."

She nodded. Then he shot at her, not without irony:

"Are you afraid of burglars?"

"They wouldn't dare touch my husband's house."

"Nor yours, now that you have inherited it."

When they got back to the living room, Maigret did not

go to the entrance but sat down again in the armchair he had previously occupied.

The couple looked at each other.

"I must point out to you that our airplane is waiting for us at Toulon."

"*Your* plane. You used the plural. Does that mean that Mori is going to fly with you?"

"Why not?"

"As a friend. With the most honorable intentions."

"It's time to change that record now. We are lovers, it's true."

"That's better."

"It's not a crime."

"Except when the husband gets a large-caliber bullet in the chest."

He turned to Mori.

"We didn't finish our little conversation on that subject just now. We were at the point where, having put on a dressing gown in a hurry, you were going to the door. You opened it, of course."

"And then?"

"I'm waiting to hear the next bit from you. Maurice Marcia didn't stay on the doorsill."

"Did I tell you it was he?"

"Let's say you didn't deny it. He didn't sit down in the living room and have a chat. On the contrary, he went right through it to the bedroom.

"He only needed to lift up the sheet to find his wife as naked as a worm. . . ."

"What delicacy!" said Line ironically.

"In fact, from the moment he came in he knew what he was going to do. He knew it when he left the Sardine."

"He had known about it for three years."

"No. You won't make me believe that he was a com-
plaisant husband, or that he was impotent. He probably
had his gun in his hand. You, Mori, you had your gun in the
pocket of your dressing gown. Where did you get it from?"

"I had no gun in the apartment."

"In that case, who did the shooting? Marcia's gun wasn't
used. As for the gun that killed him, it's probably at the
bottom of the Seine."

"You should send skin-divers down for it, then."

Maigret followed his line of thought without letting himself be discouraged.

"Supposing you went to the door without a gun, which is
possible. . . ."

"At last!"

"I haven't finished. You picked up a gun when you saw
Marcia going to the bedroom. Unless the gun was in the
bedside table and some good soul handed it to you so that
you could defend yourself."

"I'd like to hear you tell that to the jury at the trial."

"There's another possibility. . . ."

"What is it? You're making me curious."

"That it wasn't you who killed him."

"So someone else came on the scene after betraying us."

"No. Line had all the time in the world, when you went
to the door, to get the gun that was in the bedside table.
And when Marcia threatened you, she . . ."

"She would certainly have hit the ceiling, because she
has never used a firearm in her life."

"We'll talk about that later."

"In Paris, right."

"This time it will be in my office."

"Why not?"

"You may come out of it in handcuffs."

"It's not very elegant of you to try to impress me. And if I should leave France before that?"

"Interpol would waste no time finding you. You forget you have a record, and besides, you're quite conspicuous.

"I suppose you intend to get married after some time has passed?"

"It's possible."

"Go and catch your plane, then."

Manuel joked:

"Don't you want a seat?"

Maigret looked at him with the calm he had had all afternoon, and one could sense that it was the calm preceding the storm.

He had bouillabaisse in a tidy little restaurant, alone in his corner. He didn't get as much pleasure from it as he had hoped. That must have been due to his state of mind.

Night had fallen. The tree-lined promenades along the sea were softly lit and one could hear the gentle swish of the waves.

He sat down on a bench. The air was soft. He felt lazy. It wouldn't have taken much for him to have had Madame Maigret come from Paris, and they would have spent a week's holiday in Bandol.

He went to bed early and fell asleep immediately. He had to get up early the next day to get his plane at Marseilles, and he landed at Orly at ten thirty.

He took a taxi and had it take him home first. His wife did not welcome him with a great show of pleasure, but one could tell from her beaming face that she had come alive again.

"You aren't too tired?"

"A little."

"Would you like me to make some coffee for you?"

"No, thank you. I have to go to the Quai."

"Still this dratted case?"

"This dratted case, as you say."

"The papers yesterday spoke of you. They say you're being mysterious, that you are worried, even discouraged, and that you are certainly hiding something."

"If they only knew the truth! I don't know if I'll be back for lunch. That depends on what's waiting for me at the office. By the way, we must go to Bandol together sometime."

He got into the taxi parked in front of the building and a little later he climbed up the big stairway at the Quai. On his desk were already piled administrative documents, reports, and several letters. He opened the door of the inspectors' office and called Janvier.

"Had a good trip, Chief?"

"Not bad. Guess who was in the villa even before Madame Marcia?"

"Mori, of course."

"Exactly. He's a hard case, I assure you, and he'll lead us by the nose before we get him to tell us anything."

"I have some good news for you. Well, half good. Inspector Louis phoned this morning. He missed the Flea by a few hours and he wants to talk to you about it. He'll stay in his office all morning so that you can phone him."

"Do that for me. Tell him I'll go and see him."

He went and stood in front of the window and rediscovered "his" Paris with as much joy as if he had been away from it for weeks. There was a feeling of storm in the air, but it probably wouldn't break before evening.

"He's waiting for you."

"Are you coming with me? We can talk on the way."

And he did indeed, while they were going, put Janvier in the picture about everything that had happened in Bandol. They stopped for a moment in front of the police station on Place Saint-Georges, and Monsieur Louis, as some people called him formally, to tease him, joined them in the car straight away.

"Do you want to see the last place where he was hiding?"

"Yes."

"Then stop right up at the top of Montmartre, on Place du Tertre."

There were painters all along the sidewalks, and the little tables with red-checked tablecloths were ready for the tourists.

"Turn the corner into Rue du Mont-Cenis and park the car at the curb."

Farther down the street there were modern apartment houses but on the height most houses had kept their old-fashioned character. Inspector Louis took them into an alleyway between two buildings, where there was a glass-fronted workshop at the end.

Louis knocked. A loud voice cried:

"Come in!"

They found themselves in a sculptor's studio, and the sculptor was looking at the superintendent with his eyes half closed, as he would have looked at a model.

"You, you're Superintendent Maigret. Am I wrong?"

"You're not wrong."

"What about him?"

"Inspector Janvier."

"It's years since I've had so many people in my studio."

He had white hair, a little beard, and a white mustache, and his cheeks were as red as a baby's.

"Monsieur Sorel is the oldest artist on the Butte," explained Inspector Louis. "How many years did you tell me you've been in this studio?"

"Fifty-three years. I've seen them come and go, artists, starting with Picasso, with whom I often had a bite to eat. . . ."

He had a rather naïve, childish look. Looking around the studio, one couldn't have any illusions about his talent. He only sculpted children's heads, the head of the same child, one would have said, with different expressions, and undoubtedly these busts were sold at the art dealer's on Place du Tertre.

"I believe you've had the Flea with you."

"For two days and two nights. He left yesterday evening, at nightfall. He didn't dare stay any longer in the same place for fear of being seen."

"How did he happen to choose your studio?"

"What if I were to tell you that I knew him when he was only fifteen? He was a street urchin then, fending for himself as best he could, and not often getting enough to fill his belly.

"Meeting him one day on Place du Tertre, I asked him if he would like to pose for me, and he came. I remember the bust I made of him, one of my best. It's now in God knows what collection. Because of his grimaces and his enormous mouth I made a clown more real than if I'd had a professional clown as a model.

"He was a good boy. From time to time he would knock on my door, especially in the winter, and ask if he could sleep on my mattress. It was my dog's mattress, because I had a dog then, a big Saint Bernard, but that's another story."

"Did he tell you about his troubles?"

"He asked me if I could hide him for a night or two. I

107

wanted to know if he was hiding from the police. He told me that, on the contrary, he was on excellent terms with Inspector Louis and Superintendent Maigret. He added that that was precisely why some people were trying to get hold of him."

"He didn't tell you where he was going when he left here?"

"No. As far as I could tell, it's not far away. He doesn't appear to want to go far from this area."

"During those two days, he didn't talk to you about anyone in particular?"

"Yes, he did. A former policeman, now retired, who was good to him when he was a boy. I don't know his name. I don't know him at all. I only go out of my studio to do my marketing, less than a hundred yards from here, and to take my work to the dealer."

Only then did he seem to notice that they were all standing.

"Forgive me for not asking you to sit down, but I haven't enough chairs or stools. And as for offering you a drink, I have only common red wine, the same stuff Utrillo drank, which would probably be too strong for you."

"During those two days and nights, did he go out?"

"No. But he was surprised and very happy to find that I have a telephone. He called a woman to tell her how he was, and I smoked my pipe discreetly in the courtyard.

"All I can tell you is that he was terribly scared. He couldn't keep still. He jumped up at every noise, and he asked me at least ten times if I ever had any visitors. Who would come to see me? I don't even want a cleaning woman."

Maigret warmed to him, for he was indeed one of the rare specimens still living of old Montmartre.

"Oh! He mentioned you. It seems you ought to arrest

someone. But he doesn't understand why you are taking so long.

" 'If the superintendent doesn't hurry, he'll have no one for a witness, because they'll have got me before then.' "

As he went out, after shaking hands with the old man, Maigret muttered to himself:

"A retired policeman."

"I've already begun to work on that track," said Inspector Louis with his habitual impassiveness. "It's likely to be a policeman from the 18th *arrondissement*, or perhaps the 9th, because he wouldn't have come so far to live . . . appears, too, that that's the neighborhood the Flea frequented most when he was a boy.

"I have begun to study the lists of policemen who retired in the last ten years. I haven't found any yet who live in Montmartre, but I'll go on with it this afternoon."

It would have been easier, obviously, in a district where everyone knew everyone else, to ask the first old lady they met, or the grocer, but might that not have been dangerous for the Flea?

"Where shall I drop you?"

"Nowhere. I'm going to stay around here."

He had his methods. He was a sort of retriever and he would have been unhappy if he had had to work in a team. Undoubtedly he was going to go the rounds of the bars again, drowning his stomach in quarter-bottles of Vichy while listening to the conversations around him.

"To Blanche Pigoud's, Rue Fromentin."

Maigret too was beginning to worry about the fate of the Flea, but it wouldn't have done any good to put ten men, or twenty, to look for him.

"By the way, are the Mori brothers still being followed?"

"The detectives are taking turns. While his brother was away, Jo spent a lot of time on Rue du Caire, then he went off in a truck, and the detective lost him. He came back, without any crates, at about eight in the evening. He closed the steel door and went back to his apartment to have a shower and change. Do you know where he had dinner?"

"Yes. At the Sardine."

"How did you guess?"

"Because it was already a sort of take-over."

"What about Manuel?"

"Even easier. He dined at the Sardine too, with Line. It's probably the first time she had eaten in her husband's restaurant. Poor Marcia didn't guess she would soon be the owner."

"You'd think they were behaving like this out of defiance. I'm sure the staff was indignant to see her on the day of the funeral with the Mori brothers."

"Manuel doesn't give a damn what the staff think. If the employees leave, he'll replace them by his own men. That's probably his intention. I'll bet he slept at Rue Ballu."

"You win your bet. As far as I know, he's still there."

"There's something wrong somewhere," Maigret thought out loud.

"The Flea?"

"The Flea's no use to us unless we can get our hands on him. No! There's a flaw somewhere else and I'm getting a headache from trying to work it out."

"Shall I come up with you?"

"Better not. In spite of her profession, the girl is quite shy. With me, she's already at ease, but if we both go . . ."

This time the Flea's girl friend was up, having her breakfast by the window.

"A cup of coffee? It's ready."

"All right, then."

110

She seemed worried.

"I know where he spent the last two nights, but he went off yesterday evening."

"What district was he in?"

"Near Place du Tertre, with an old sculptor."

"That's funny. He told me about him once when we went to have dinner just below the Sacré Coeur. It reminded him of his childhood. He described the mattress on which he used to sleep, which had belonged to a big dog."

"He didn't talk to you about anyone else in the neighborhood?"

"I don't remember. I don't think so."

"A former policeman, for example?"

"No, really, that means nothing to me."

"Has he called you?"

"Twice."

"What did he say?"

"He's getting more and more scared. He doesn't understand why you aren't arresting the Mori brothers. Their gang would keep quiet then and Justin would be able to feel free."

"Is he angry with me?"

"A little, I think, yes. He's angry with Inspector Louis, too. I told him what you said to me."

"Listen. There's every chance he may call you again, unless there's no telephone where he is. Tell him to call me. I'll give him all the assurances he wants."

"Is that true?"

"I need to see him, and it is probable that two hours after that, the Mori brothers will be behind bars."

"I'll tell him. I'll do what I can. Put yourself in my place. He doesn't believe in anything, or anyone, any more."

111

A quarter of an hour later, Maigret and Janvier were sitting at the bar in the Sardine. It was the time when they set the tables for lunch and the headwaiter, by the cash desk, was taking telephone reservations.

"A beer, Freddy. . . ."

"What about you?" Freddy asked Janvier.

"The same."

"We don't have anything but imported beer."

"It doesn't matter."

It looked as though he were serving them against his will, and he glanced frequently at the door, as if he were afraid to see one of the Mori brothers come in.

"I've never seen so many people at a funeral," murmured Maigret, as if to force him to speak.

"There were a lot of people, yes."

"And there were almost as many in Bandol. People from everywhere, Nice, Cannes, Toulon, Marseilles . . . And the cars! I counted no fewer than five Ferraris."

To keep himself in countenance, Freddy was wiping the glasses. Comitat, the headwaiter, had put down the telephone and instead of coming over to them, he stayed at the other end of the room, with all the signs of ignoring them.

Maigret said, with irony:

"Chilly in here today."

The temperature must have been between seventy-seven and eighty-two degrees.

"Yes, it's chilly."

"Well, have you seen the boss yet?"

"What boss?"

"Line Marcia. She had dinner here last night with the Mori brothers. Of course Manuel's really the boss. . . ."

"Listen, Monsieur Maigret, I don't meddle in your affairs. Don't you meddle in things here. First of all, if anyone sees me talking to you, that could be bad for me. It might also not do you any good."

The superintendent and Janvier looked at each other.

"Will you wait here a moment, Janvier?"

And he went off in the direction of the toilets. To get to them, he had to pass near Comitat.

"Good morning, Monsieur Raoul," he said.

"Freddy should have told you you're not welcome here."

"He did. Change of management. And suddenly everyone in the place is jittery."

"I'd be obliged if you wouldn't come back again."

"You're forgetting it's a public place and it's open to anyone who is decently dressed and has enough money."

He went to the men's room, and back to the bar. It was a little after quarter past twelve.

"You know what we're going to do, Janvier? We're going to have lunch here."

They went toward the nearest table. Comitat rushed up.

"I'm sorry, but this table is taken."

"Then we'll take the next one."

"It's taken too. All the tables are taken."

"Let's say, in that case, that this one is taken by me. Sit down, Janvier."

It wasn't malice on Maigret's part. He was furious, and he wanted to make them fume in their turn.

"The menu, please. And don't forget that I can have this place closed in twenty-four hours."

The menu was enormous, with the wine list on the verso.

"There are *coquilles Saint-Jacques*, Janvier. What do you say to that?"

"*Coquilles Saint-Jacques*, fine."

"Followed by braised rib of beef."

"That's fine too."

113

He handed back the menu.

"A light wine . . . a Beaujolais?"

"Fine with me."

The headwaiter stood behind them as straight as a ramrod. Then four customers came in and sat down near the window. The little dark cashier had taken her seat, but Maigret tried in vain to catch her eye. She appeared not to recognize him.

Monsieur Maurice was dead. When he was alive no one made a wrong move, but there was still something mellow in the atmosphere.

Last night Mori had come to take possession of the place, in the company of Madame Marcia, and they had all understood.

From now on they would all have to watch their steps. They had started to do so. They just managed to mumble a few words when their paths crossed.

"What do you bet we won't be served inside half an hour, if not an hour?"

And in fact the table for four was served before them, then two English people who had only just come in. The room filled up bit by bit, and the more they delayed in serving them, the more Maigret smiled, smoking his pipe ostentatiously.

"Don't hurry!" He said to the headwaiter, who was passing.

"No, monsieur. I don't intend to."

The Moris did not turn up, and the two men finally had something to eat and drink.

6

When Maigret got back to the Quai it was after three
o'clock, and the first person he saw was the inescapable Inspector Louis sitting on one of the benches in the corridor,
his black hat on his knees.

The superintendent had him come into his office, and
Louis sat down once more on the edge of a chair.

"I think I've been lucky, Superintendent."

He had the soft voice of a shy man, and he rarely looked the person he was speaking to in the face.

"When I left you this morning, I began to go around the bars and cafés again, at the top of Montmartre, around Place du Tertre. I know it's a mania of mine. I came to the Trois Tonneaux, a *bistrot* on Rue Gabrielle. I stayed at the counter as usual, and I took my customary quarter-bottle of Vichy."

Maigret knew that it would be no use to hurry him. The inspector spoke with the slowness and care for exactitude that were part of his character.

"In a corner, under a clock with an advertisement on it, four men were playing *belote*. They were all fairly old, and they had probably been playing their game in the same place, at the same time, for many years.

"I jumped when I heard one of them say:

" 'Your turn, officer.'

"The man he was talking to must have been between seventy and seventy-five, but he was still youthful.

"Three times, in the space of ten minutes, they spoke to him, calling him officer.

" 'Was he a policeman?' I asked the proprietor in a low voice.

" 'He was for forty years. An old-style policeman. He was a familiar figure in the district, and he was like a father to the children.'

" 'Has he been retired for long?'

" 'Ten years at least, and he comes in every day for his game. He lives alone, now that his son is married and has moved to Meaux. His daughter is a nurse at the Bichat Hospital and there's another son, I don't know what he does, nothing particularly good, I think.'

" 'Does he live far from here?'

" 'Not very far. On Rue Tholozé. Right opposite the only dance hall in the street. His wife died five years ago and he does his own cooking and cleaning. We have a lot of them around here, old men and women who live alone on a small pension.' "

Maigret knew Montmartre well enough to know that it is a town within a town. Some people never went beyond Place Clichy.

"Have you got his exact address?"

"I left the *bistrot* so that I wouldn't attract attention. The man came out half an hour later and stopped at the butcher's to buy two chops.

"I followed him to Rue Tholozé, at some distance, because he would be able to tell a tail. He went into a three-story building just opposite the Tam-Tam, a dance hall. I called the police station of the 18th *arrondissement* to ask for the help of a detective for an hour or two. One of the young ones came, and he is keeping watch not far from the house."

Now he was silent. He had said everything, in his own way.

"Did you hear that, Janvier?"

For Janvier had come into the office at the same time as the superintendent.

"Shall we go?"

"Of course."

"Shall we take any men with us?"

"There's no point. We have to carry it off as discreetly as possible."

They took one of the little black cars that were parked in the courtyard of the Criminal Police.

"Rue Tholozé isn't a one-way street, is it?"

"It can't be, because it ends in a flight of steps."

From a distance they saw the young policeman standing well away from the house.

"I'll go in alone," said Maigret. "There's no point in scaring him."

He spoke to the concierge, showing his police badge.

"Is the officer at home?"

"Monsieur Colson? Of course everyone still calls him officer. He came in about two hours ago. He's probably taking his nap now."

"What floor?"

"Second floor, the door on the left."

There was no elevator, of course. It was an old house, like almost all the houses on the street, and a thick smell of cooking hung in the stairwell.

There was no doorbell, and Maigret knocked at the door.

"Come in," said a deep voice.

It was a small apartment, filled with furniture that had once furnished an entire house. In the bedroom on the right there were two beds, one of which had undoubtedly been used by successive children.

There were two, or three, of everything. There was no icebox, but a wire-netted meat safe hung out of the window.

"It isn't possible! Superintendent Maigret in my house! Come in, please. There's someone here who'll be very happy to see you."

He showed the superintendent into a stuffy room which served as both dining room and living room. A man not quite five feet tall, who looked like a child whose face had been accidentally lined, was looking anxiously at the visitor.

"Have you arrested him?" he asked before anything else.

"Not yet, but you're safe."

Officer Colson interrupted.

"I've told him at least ten times that he ought to call you

118

and tell you where he was. He was trembling when he came here. He is terrified of those Mori brothers, is that their name? They were unknown in my time."

"They're barely thirty years old."

"I watch TV in the evening, but I don't take any papers. Justin remembered me. I knew him when he hung about this neighborhood, when he had only old espadrilles on his feet."

"What are you going to do with me?"

The Flea was tense and could not relax.

"We'll both go to the Quai des Orfèvres. In my office we'll talk, just you and I. Most probably, after we have talked, the Mori brothers will be arrested."

"How did you find me?"

"It was Inspector Louis who got on your trail."

"The others could have done as much."

"Thank you for the hospitality you've given him, officer, and I hope the chops were good."

"How did you know . . .?"

"Inspector Louis again. And have a good game of *belote* tomorrow morning!"

He turned to the midget, who still hadn't relaxed.

"Come on."

The retired policeman took them to the door and watched them go downstairs, not without a certain melancholy.

"Get into the car."

The Flea found himself in the back with Inspector Louis.

"And I thought I was so well hidden," Justin sighed.

"It was only by chance that I got on the trail of the officer."

He kept as far away from the door as possible, afraid of being seen from outside.

They went up the stairs together at Criminal Police headquarters. The Flea looked at them with a kind of respect

119

tinged with fear. Maigret wondered which course to take—
to have all three of them in his office, or to question Justin
Crotton alone.

He decided on the latter course.

"I'll see you shortly," he said to Louis and Janvier.
"Come on in."

He stopped himself just in time from saying "boy."

"Sit down. Do you smoke?"

"Yes."

"Have you got any cigarettes?"

"I have two left."

"Take this pack."

Maigret always had two or three packs in his drawer for
interviews.

"What do you. . .?"

"Just a minute."

For there was a note on his desk.

"The laboratory would like you to phone them."

He called Moers.

"You've got something?"

"Yes. The laboratory has done a fine job. The textile
man went to the best rug dealer in Paris. His first impres-
sions were confirmed. The silk threads come from an old
Chinese rug. It must date from the sixteenth or seventeenth
century. There can't be any more than three or four outside
museums in France.

"The dealer doesn't know who owns them. He's going to
check on it. There's something else more important. There
were tiny traces of blood on the carpet, where the rug had
been. The blood was very diluted with water. They must
have washed and rewashed the stain, with a teasel brush,
because they also found a piece of teasel."

"Is it possible to tell what blood group it belongs to?"

"That's been done. Group A."

"Unfortunately, no one thought of checking Monsieur Maurice's blood group before it was too late. Unless the medical examiner . . ."

"Yes. Perhaps he thought of it. Have you had his report?"

"He doesn't mention it."

The Flea was looking at the superintendent as if he couldn't quite believe what was happening to him. But why couldn't he relax? What was he still afraid of?

Maigret opened the door.

"Janvier, try to get on to the medical examiner as fast as you can. Ask him for me if he thought of establishing Marcia's blood group. If he hasn't done so, get him to tell you what they did with his clothes."

There were about twenty inspectors typing reports, and in the middle of them Louis was sitting erect on a chair, his hat on his knees.

Back in his office, the superintendent spoke to the Flea.

"Now let's see. What time is it? Four o'clock. It's likely we'll find your friend at home."

And in fact he did hear Blanche Pigoud's voice on the other end of the line.

"Is that you, Justin?"

"No. This is Superintendent Maigret."

"Have you any news?"

"He's in my office."

"Did he go there on his own accord?"

"No. I had to look for him."

"Where was he?"

"In Montmartre, as I expected."

"Have you arrested the . . .?"

"The Mori brothers. No. One thing at a time. Here's Justin."

He signaled him to take the receiver.

"Hello. Is that you?"

He was awkward, overcome.

"I don't know yet. I've hardly been here for a quarter of an hour, and no one's asked me any questions yet. Yes, I'm well. No, I don't know when I'll be back. Good-by."

"You won't have to wait long for him," Maigret said, taking the receiver which was held out to him. "You needn't worry any more, anyway."

After hanging up, he smoked his pipe slowly, watching Justin Crotton carefully. He could not understand the nervousness the Flea still showed.

"Do you always tremble like that?"

"No."

"What are you afraid of in my office now? Of me?"

"Perhaps."

"Why?"

"Because you frighten me. Everything to do with the police frightens me."

"And yet you turned to a former policeman to find a refuge."

"As far as I'm concerned, Officer Colson isn't a real policeman. I knew him when I was hardly sixteen, and it's thanks to him that I was never charged with vagrancy."

"While I . . .?"

"You're so important."

"How did you know that Line Marcia was Manuel's mistress?"

"Everyone in the *boîtes* in the district knew."

"And for three years Monsieur Maurice knew nothing?"

"It looks that way."

"You aren't sure?"

"It's always the person concerned who doesn't know anything, isn't it? Monsieur Maurice was a rich, influential man. I don't think anyone would have dared to say to his face:

"'Your wife is deceiving you with one of your friends.'"

"Were Marcia and the Mori brothers friends?"

"For some years, yes."

"How do you know?"

"Because the Mori brothers went regularly to the Sardine and Monsieur Maurice would sit at their table. They would stay there after it closed."

"Did they visit him in his private apartment?"

"I've seen them go there several times."

"When Marcia was at home?"

"Yes."

"How do you know all that?"

"Because I walk around Montmartre a lot. I have big ears. I listen to what people are saying. Nobody pays any attention to me."

"Did you often go to the Sardine?"

"To the bar, yes. Freddy is almost a buddy of mine."

"I don't think he will be any more."

"On the night of the murder I was on Rue Fontaine when Monsieur Maurice rushed out suddenly, at a time that was quite unusual for him."

"What time was that?"

"Just after midnight. He didn't take his car, and he ran to Square La Bruyère."

"Did you know his wife was in Manuel's apartment?"

"Yes."

"How did you know that she was there that particular evening?"

"Because I had followed her there."

"In fact, your passion is to follow people and watch them?"

"I've always dreamed of being a policeman. My height cut that out. Also perhaps my lack of education."

"Right. You're following Monsieur Maurice. He goes into Manuel's. Was there any light in the windows?"

"Yes."

"How long had Line been there?"

"About an hour."

"You didn't go into the building?"

"No."

"Did you know what was going to happen?"

"Yes. Except I didn't know which one of them would be killed."

"Did you hear the shot?"

"No. Nor did the other tenants, unless they thought it was a car backfiring."

"Go on."

"After about a quarter of an hour Madame Marcia came out of the house and hurried back home."

"Did you follow her?"

"No. I thought I'd stay."

"What happened then?"

"A car came rushing up and I was almost caught. It was the other Mori brother, Jo. His brother must have phoned him to come around in a hurry."

Maigret was following this recital with increasing interest. Up to this point, no flaw in the story had turned up, but he had a vaguely uneasy feeling nevertheless.

"And then?"

"The two men went out, carrying a rolled-up rug that had something heavy in it."

"Marcia's body?"

"Almost certainly. They heaved it into the car and dashed off in the direction of Place Constantin-Pecqueur. I didn't have a car and I couldn't follow them."

"What did you do?"

"I stayed there, waiting."

"Were they away for long?"

"About half an hour."

"Did they bring the rug back?"

"No. I never saw it again. They both went up to the apartment and Jo didn't come out till an hour later."

Everything fitted. The two men had first taken the body to the darkest part of Avenue Junot. As for the rug, they had probably thrown it into the Seine.

Coming back to Square La Bruyère, they had carefully removed all trace of what had happened.

"What did you do then?"

"I waited until the next day to call Inspector Louis."

"Why him and not the police station, for example, or the Criminal Police?"

"Because that scares me."

And he was really scared.

"It wasn't the first time you had phoned him."

"No. I've been giving him information that way for a long time. I know him by sight. We go to the same places. He's always alone."

"Why did you disappear?"

"Because I was afraid the Mori brothers would think it was I."

Maigret frowned. That was the least convincing part of the Flea's statement.

"Why would they have thought of you? Had you had any dealings with them?"

"No. But they've seen me in bars. They know I wander all over Montmartre and that I know a lot."

"That's not it," Maigret said suddenly.

The Flea looked at him with surprise and then with fear.

"What do you mean?"

"It would have taken more than that for them to decide to kill you."

"I swear . . ."

"You've never spoken to them?"

" Never. You only have to ask them."

He was lying, and Maigret knew it, without having any proof.

"Well, we'll arrest them. While you're waiting, come with me into the office next door.

"Stay in here quietly and wait for me. Perhaps one of the inspectors has a newspaper he'll lend you."

"I don't like to read."

"All right. Don't worry."

Maigret signaled to Janvier to follow him into his office.

"Did you get the Medico-Legal Institute?"

"I got Doctor Bourdet himself on the phone. His clothes and underwear were still there. The blood is group A."

"The same as they found on the carpet."

"It seems it's the most common group in this country."

"I'm going up to see the magistrate and then I'll doubtless need you and Lucas. Lapointe too."

Maigret found himself again in the long hallway along which were the magistrates' chambers; almost all the benches were occupied by people who were waiting their turn to be called. Some of them, sitting between two policemen, were handcuffed. Others were accused but still free, or were witnesses, and had a less glassy look.

Maigret knocked at Judge Bouteille's door, went in, and found the magistrate dictating to his clerk.

"Excuse me."

"Sit down. It's only administrative stuff, anyway. Have you used my warrants?"

"Only the search warrant. An old Chinese rug has disappeared from the bedroom of the elder Mori brother. The carpet underneath had several spots that have been shown to be spots of blood. Group A. Now Marcia's clothes, examined by Doctor Bourdet, have blood of the same group around the hole made by the shot."

"That's not proof, you understand."

"It's an indication. There is another indication. Since the afternoon of the funeral, Mori has slept at Rue Ballu, and the two brothers have virtually taken over the Sardine."

"Have you found that midget? What's his nickname again?"

"The Flea. He's downstairs, with a good guard on him. He confirms that a little after midnight he saw Monsieur Maurice go into the building on Square La Bruyère where the elder Mori lives. A quarter of an hour later, Line Marcia came out of it and rushed home. Finally the younger Mori came up in a car, as if called in as reinforcements by telephone.

"Half an hour later the two brothers went downstairs, carrying a heavy bundle that they dumped in the car.

"The Flea couldn't follow them to Avenue Junot, since he had no car, but he's certain. The body was wrapped in a multicolored rug."

"Do you intend to arrest them?"

"This afternoon. I would like another warrant, however, in the home of Madame Line Marcia."

"Do you think she . . . ?"

"She's certainly an accomplice. I suspect her of having handed the gun to her lover. I even wonder if it wasn't she who fired the shot."

The magistrate turned to his clerk.

"You heard. Make out the warrant. I have an idea that they'll be hard to crack."

"I expect so too. And it would be imprudent to bring

them to trial without solid proof, because they'll pay for
not only the best lawyers in Paris but also all the false witnesses they'll need."

A little later Maigret went back into his office and did
something he didn't usually do. He took his gun out of the
drawer and put it in his pocket.

Then he called Lucas, Janvier, and Lapointe.

"Come on, boys. This time it's all or nothing. You, Janvier, come with me. Go and get your gun, because we must
be prepared for anything with these people.

"You two as well," he said to Lucas and Lapointe. "You
go to Rue du Caire. There's every chance that you'll find
young Mori there. If not, try his suite in the Hôtel des Iles,
on Avenue Trudaine. Finally, if he isn't there either, try the
Sardine. Here's the warrant for him. Take a pair of handcuffs. You too, Janvier."

They separated in the courtyard and the two cars went
toward their separate destinations.

"Where are we going?"

"To Manuel's place first."

The concierge told them that he wasn't in, but that the
cleaning woman certainly was. They went up. The cleaning
woman was horribly thin, and one wondered how she
managed to stay on her feet. She was about sixty and she
must have been ill. The expression on her face was bitter
and aggressive.

"What do you want?"

"Monsieur Manuel Mori."

"He isn't here."

"When did he go out?"

"I don't know."

"He didn't sleep in his bed, did he?"

"That's none of your business."

"Police."

"Police or not, it's no concern of yours what bed a man sleeps in."

"Have you noticed that the rug that was in the bedroom has disappeared?"

"So what? If he made a hole in it with a cigarette and sent it to be repaired, that's his business."

"Is your employer nice to you?"

"Like a prison wall."

They were well suited to each other.

"Well, are you going to stay there? I'm going on with my vacuuming, because I haven't any time to waste."

A few minutes later, the two men stopped in front of the late Marcia's house.

"Is Madame Marcia upstairs?" Maigret asked the concierge.

"I don't think she has gone out. Though it's always possible to go out the garden door, which is always open."

"Night and day?"

"Yes."

"So you don't know who goes in and comes out?"

"Very few tenants use that door."

"I have the impression she wasn't alone last night."

"I had that impression too."

"Have you seen a man go out this morning?"

"No. He's probably still up there. According to the maid, we can expect him to be the new tenant."

"Whom was the maid more loyal to?"

"More to Monsieur Maurice."

"Thank you."

Maigret and Janvier went up to the first floor. Maigret rang and several minutes passed before anyone answered.

"Madame Marcia, please."

"I don't know if she can see you. But come in."

She showed them into the big living room, which had gone back to its former appearance.

"We must come back here with experts in antiques," Maigret murmured.

Instead of Line, it was Manuel Mori who appeared in the doorway.

"You again!"

"I asked to see Line Marcia."

"She doesn't want to see you, and I'm going to stop you from bothering her."

"I'm going to bother you both, however. In the name of the law, I arrest you."

"Oh, the famous warrant."

"This time there's another one, in the name of Line Marcia, née Polin."

"You dared . . ."

"I dared, and I advise you not to make any trouble. That could have serious consequences for you."

Manuel made as if to put his hand to his pocket, where the shape of a gun could be seen. Maigret said softly:

"Put your hands down, boy."

Line's lover was pale.

"Keep him covered, Janvier."

Maigret himself looked for a bell and he found one near the massive fireplace. He pressed it. Some moments later the maid stopped, disconcerted, in the doorway.

"Go and get Madame Marcia for me. Tell her to bring some clothes, underwear, and toilet articles sufficient for several days."

She came a few minutes later, her hands empty.

"What does this . . .?"

She stopped, seeing Janvier's gun.

"Here is a warrant in your name. I've come to arrest you both."

"But it's nothing to do with me!"

"You were at least an accomplice in the murder, and you tried to cover up for the one who was responsible. That's called aiding and abetting."

"If every time a woman has a lover, she risks . . ."

"Not all lovers shoot the husband. Go and get some things. Just a minute. Give me your gun, Manuel."

Manuel hesitated. His expression grew hard, and Maigret was prepared for anything, staring him straight in the eye.

Finally a hand held out the gun to him.

"Stay with him, Janvier. I don't like to leave the woman alone. I'm not sure that I'd find her again."

"I have to change."

"You won't be the first woman I've seen change. How much did you use to wear when you danced at the Tabarin?"

The atmosphere was heavy and menace hung in the air. Maigret followed Line to the end of the hall and she went into a pearl-gray and yellow room with Louis XVI furniture. The bed was unmade. On a little table there were a bottle of whiskey and two glasses, half full.

He believed her capable of anything, even of grabbing the bottle and smashing it over his head.

He poured her a large drink of whiskey and put the bottle out of her reach.

"Don't you want any?"

"No. Get yourself ready."

"How long do you think we'll be away? Or rather, will I be away?"

"That depends."

"On whom?"

"On you and on the magistrate."

"What has made you decide to arrest us all of a sudden, when yesterday there was no question of it?"

"Let's say that since yesterday we have made some important discoveries."

"You certainly haven't found the gun that killed my husband."

"You know very well it's in the Seine, together with the blood-soaked rug."

"What prison are you going to take us to?"

"To the Central Police Station first, in the basement of the Law Courts."

"Isn't that where they put the prostitutes?"

"Sometimes."

"And you dare . . ."

Maigret pointed to the bed.

"You haven't even given this bed time to get cold."

"You're a horrible man."

"For the moment, yes. Hurry up."

She stripped all at once, purposely, as if she wanted to provoke him.

"I want to take a shower. There can't be any where I'm going."

She had the lovely, supple body of a dancer. But the superintendent wasn't moved at all.

"I'll give you five minutes."

And he stood in the doorway of the bathroom, which had another door.

It took her nearly a quarter of an hour to get ready. She put on the same black coat that she had worn the previous evening, the same white hat. She had thrown a little underwear in a small suitcase, together with some toilet articles.

"I'll go with you, since I have no choice. I hope you'll pay dearly for it."

They rejoined the two men in the living room. One could see from Manuel's surprised look that he had been wondering why his mistress had made them wait so long. Did he, too, know that she was capable of anything?

"The handcuffs, Janvier."

"Are you going to put handcuffs on me?" asked Manuel, who had turned white and already had his fist up.

He was much stronger than Janvier, but a long look from Maigret made him lower his fist, and the handcuffs clicked on.

"I hope you aren't going to put them on her too."

"Only if it becomes necessary."

The maid saw them to the door, a queer smile on her lips.

"Down you go."

He had Mori get into the back of the car and sit there with him, while the woman sat in the front with Janvier. Neither of them tried to escape, which would have been futile, anyway.

"What about my brother?"

"He should be at the Criminal Police already. Unless they've had difficulty getting hold of him."

"Did you send your men to Rue du Caire?"

"Yes."

"He should have been there. My brother has nothing to do with it. I didn't even see him that night."

"You're lying."

"You'll have to prove the contrary."

The car went into the courtyard and all four climbed the stairs.

"Into my office, Janvier."

The window was still open. The storm seemed close now,

and one would have sworn it was already raining in Montparnasse.

"Sit down, both of you. Janvier, see if Lucas and Lapointe are back."

The inspector came back a moment later.

"He's next door, under heavy guard."

"Have him come in."

Jo was as furious as his elder brother.

"I'll put in a complaint."

"That's fine. You tell that to the magistrate."

"How long are you going to keep us here?"

"That depends on the jury. One of you risks twenty years or more. You, you'll have a few years, anyway."

"I haven't done anything."

"I know you didn't fire the shot, but I also know that when your brother phoned you in the middle of the night, you helped him to take Marcia's body in your car and dump it on Avenue Junot."

"That's a lie."

"Janvier! Bring in the person waiting next door."

"If it's he . . ."

"It is he, exactly. Come in, Justin. Sit down."

Janvier remained standing, as if keeping guard, while Lapointe, seated at the end of the desk, took the interrogation down in shorthand.

"Is that what you call a witness?" grumbled Manuel, more snarling than ever. "You can buy him for a hundred francs and he'll say anything you want him to."

Maigret pretended not to have heard and turned toward Line.

"Will you tell me, madame, if on the night of Monday to Tuesday you were in the apartment of Manuel Mori, this man here, on Square La Bruyère?"

"That's none of your business."

"Am I to conclude from your attitude that you have decided not to answer any questions?"

"That depends on the questions."

Her lover looked at her, frowning.

"However, you admit being the mistress of this man?"

"I am the mistress of whom I like, and as far as I know there's no article in the Code Napoléon that forbids it."

"Where did you sleep last night?"

"At home."

"With whom?"

"As I said . . ."

"Did you know that your lover had a gun in or on his bedside table?"

"No comment."

"I must insist on that question, in your own interest, because it is very important. Particularly for you.

"When your husband rang the doorbell you were in bed, naked, under the bedclothes. Manuel slipped on a dressing gown to go and open the door, but he didn't pick up his gun.

"Your husband had a gun in his hand. He went straight to the bedroom and pulled back the sheet. What he said to you, I don't know. He turned to Manuel at once. He moved over to the bed, and a minute afterward he had a gun in his hand. He shot first. That's the first version. In the course of the reconstruction, which will shortly take place, we'll see if it holds up.

"There is another hypothesis, just as plausible. You knew where the gun was. Your husband was about to shoot your lover and you shot first. What do you say about that?"

"I say it's pure madness. I would have had to be there first, anyway. And then . . ."

Without listening to her, Maigret turned to Manuel.

"And you, what have you to say about that?"

The elder Mori had a grim look and he shook his head.

"I have nothing to say about it."

"You don't protest against this theory?"

"I repeat, I have nothing to say."

"Are you going to give out on me like that? Well, my boy, that's not going to last long."

"You'll note I didn't say anything."

"You could have denied it, couldn't you?"

"I'll perhaps say something later, in front of the magistrate, with my lawyer there."

"And meanwhile I get it in the neck. Listen, Superintendent . . ."

She marched furiously toward Maigret's desk and began to speak and wave her arms about. It was no longer the elegant Line Marcia, but a wild animal broken loose.

7

"It's true that I was on Square La Bruyère, there's no point in denying it, becaus the concierge saw us, drunk though he was, and Manuel couldn't buy him for long with a bottle of brandy. Also, undoubtedly, my fingerprints are everywhere, and traces of powder or cream, things like that.

"For three years I've been there at least twice a week.

"And that little guttersnipe, that midget there in the corner, must have known all about it.

"As for Manuel, he knew what he was doing, becoming my lover. It wasn't I he wanted, but to step into my husband's shoes."

She had gone berserk and was talking in a jerky way.

"When Maurice first took him up he was only a washed-up little pimp. What you don't know, I'm sure, is that Maurice was the big boss."

Maigret smoked his pipe in little puffs, avoiding interrupting the flow of words. Line was talking in a rush of passion, or rather of fear. From time to time she turned to Manuel and looked at him with hatred.

And only a few hours ago they had been both lovers and accomplices.

Now it was a question of who would throw the responsibility onto the other.

"Janvier! Take his handcuffs off."

"At last! You've remembered. It would be difficult for me to escape from here, I suppose."

Manuel had lost his arrogance and was merely sneering.

The Flea remained motionless on his chair, in the corner farthest away from the Mori brothers. He still looked frightened and, even though Manuel was helpless for the moment, he still looked at him with terror.

He had been afraid of him for so long, considered him as a sort of superman, that he could not throw off his fear.

"I'll spill the beans, as they say," she went on. "We were in bed. The doorbell rang."

"You didn't expect it?"

She hesitated for a second.

"No. Why should I have expected that my husband would come that particular night?"

"He didn't know about your affair, he who knew everything that went on in Pigalle?"

"Why would he have waited for three years? If he knew about it, he was playing his game too, for he was madly jealous."

"Do you think that Manuel was expecting this visit?"

This time the silence was longer.

"Frankly, I don't know. He got up and slipped on the dressing gown that was on the back of a chair. Then he got his gun out of the drawer in the bedside table and put it in his pocket."

"She's lying, Superintendent. It's a light silk dressing gown. A gun would be seen through the material. Listen. . . . I said I would talk only in the presence of my lawyer. I'm only asking you not to believe everything this woman tells you and to check it.

"But I can tell you the truth now on one point at least. She's the one who threw herself at me when I began to go around with Maurice. She kept saying that he was an old man, that he was finished. An old crank, that's what she said."

"No, it was he who . . ."

Manuel stood up.

"Sit down."

For an impartial observer, the scene would have been almost comical. Maigret in his chair, facing a rack of pipes, was as inexpressive as a wax figure at the Musée Grévin. He watched them, observing the reactions of each one in turn.

The Flea was still trembling in his corner as if danger were threatening him personally.

The younger of the brothers was listening without interrupting. For the moment it wasn't so much the Marcia case which was being played out, but a bitter and pitiless dispute between two lovers.

"'Whenever you want, you can take over from him.' That's what she said. She's ambitious, greedy. She had begun right at the bottom of the ladder, because she'd done her stint on Place Pigalle before she worked at the Tabarin."

It was revolting, and poor Lapointe tried to hide his indignation while taking notes.

"So she already had the idea of killing him?" Maigret asked in a quiet voice, as if it was the most natural question in the world.

"At any rate, it was an idea that came to her in the first few months."

"And you dissuaded her?"

"It's not true, Superintendent. It was he who became my lover just so that he could step into my husband's shoes someday."

"Once more, didn't he suspect anything?"

"He trusted me. Besides, it was the first time I had deceived him."

"That's a lie. She's even slept with Freddy the bartender. He can tell you that."

She turned to him again, full of hate, as if she were going to spit in his face.

"Things would be easier, madame, if you would sit down once more."

"I saw how you were examining the furniture and the pictures in Rue Ballu. I'm sure you understood everything and that you're going to have them gone over by experts. They're bound to smell a rat.

"But it wasn't the idea of this shabby little man."

So Manuel had become a shabby little man!

"The château gang, as it was called, was my husband's idea, and he's the one who organized it. There were six or seven trusted men placed throughout France. He alerted them when an operation was planned, and they would come to the rendezvous given to them.

"The Mori brothers would be there with their truck and some crates for camouflage."

"What happened to the furniture and the various works of art when Maurice and Manuel had had their pick?"

"They went back to the provinces, to unlicensed antique dealers. I dare you to say that it isn't true."

"That's the only true thing she's said since we've been here, Superintendent. It's impossible to deny it, since the furniture will be gone over by experts."

"But you directed the operations."

"On the spot, yes. But the orders came from Maurice. He took no risks. In his restaurant he played the part of a reformed crook, and there were magistrates who would shake him by the hand."

"Was it a profitable business?"

"A gold mine."

"Which you tried to take over."

"It was her idea."

"Are you sure of that?"

"It's my word against hers. You can draw your own conclusions. I'm sorry I threw the gun in the Seine, for you would have found her fingerprints and not mine on it."

"Can't you see he's a cold-blooded liar?"

At the moment when it was least expected, Maigret turned to the Flea, who turned pale.

"At what time did you telephone?"

"A little before midnight," he stammered.
"What did you tell him?"
"The truth."
"What truth?"
"That his wife and Manuel were in the apartment."
"What put that idea into your head?"

Justin turned his head away, and he looked almost like a schoolboy caught out.

"Answer me."

"I don't know. . . . I wanted revenge."

"For what?"

"For everything. I tried to get into the gang two years ago. I knew how they worked. I know almost everything that goes on in Pigalle and on the Butte.

"I asked Manuel Mori to take me on, and he told me he didn't need a midget like me."

It was Manuel's turn to speak.

"He's lying."

Maigret smoked pipe after pipe, and the air was blue with smoke.

"You may smoke too," he said.

"What about me?" Line asked.

"You too."

"I haven't got any cigarettes, and I don't want any from that shit."

He held out a pack which he took out of his drawer, but he didn't go so far as to light her cigarette. Her hands were trembling so much that she had difficulty in lighting it, and she needed three matches.

"What's your version of the truth, Manuel?"

"He never asked me for anything, and I didn't even know him other than by sight. Everyone knows he's an informer."

"That's not true."

"One at a time. Your turn, Justin."

"I phoned to get even with him because he treated me like dirt."

"Where did you call from?"

"From the nearest phone booth. I could see the lights of the restaurant in the distance."

"Did you know you were going to set a crime in motion?"

"I wasn't sure."

"But the idea didn't upset you?"

"No."

"If it had been a question of someone else, would you have done the same thing?"

This question left him somewhat at a loss. He had to think.

"I don't know," he confessed.

"Weren't you taking revenge for your size and your face that these people laughed at?"

"I don't know," he repeated.

"Listen carefully to what I'm asking you now and answer carefully. You have just been lying, because you are afraid of Manuel."

Panic overtook the midget again, as if even here the Mori brothers were all-powerful.

"I've already told you the truth."

"No. The truth is that you were paid to make that telephone call at a specific time."

"Who would have paid me?"

"Manuel, of course."

"I protest," cried Manuel. "I'd like to know why I would want to get myself caught *in flagrante* by the husband of my mistress."

And finally Justin began to speak.

"He gave me a thousand francs. He threatened to kill me if I said anything. He added:

" 'I have men everywhere who will do it if I can't.'

"It hurt me to do it to Monsieur Maurice, because I liked him."

"But you did it anyway,"

"I didn't want to be shot."

"It didn't occur to you that Monsieur Maurice might have shot first?"

"From the moment that man . . ."

He pointed to Manuel.

"From the moment that man had decided how it would happen, it would happen that way. He's a kind of devil."

Maigret couldn't keep himself from smiling, and Line came into the foreground again.

"You see, Superintendent, I wasn't lying. I didn't know about the telephone call. So I wasn't waiting for my husband to come in, and therefore I didn't have a gun. . . ."

"That's not true! She lies as naturally as breathing. The phone call was her idea. I can still hear her saying to me, 'If you kill him or have him killed anywhere, they'll get you in the end, because the police will soon find out about our relationship. But supposing he catches us *in flagrante*, as they say. I know him. He won't come unarmed. He'll threaten you. Or rather, he'll threaten me. In either case it's self-defense.' "

"That doesn't prove that it wasn't you who fired the shot."

She was crying with rage.

"But what do I have to do to get you to believe me?"

"I don't have to believe you. Let me tell you again, it's the jury who will decide."

"I've never held a gun in my life."

"That's not true," interrupted Manuel. "At Bandol, I've seen her shoot seagulls."

"With a pistol?"

"With her husband's pistol."

"And did she hit them?"

"She killed several right in front of my eyes."

"Justin?"

"Yes, Superintendent."

"When and where did Manuel talk to you about the phone call?"

"The night of the murder, on Rue Pigalle. I had just taken Blanche to the Canary. I go there every night at the same time."

"Did he tell you to call about midnight?"

"Yes."

"You see!" cried Line. "I didn't even know where to find the Flea, and Manuel was careful not to tell me about the phone call."

Maigret was thirsty. He would have given a lot to have beer brought up, but he would have had to order for everybody.

He had got an important result, the most important. The two lovers, attacking each other, were no longer denying the murder of Monsieur Maurice in the apartment on Square La Bruyère.

As to which of the two was the guilty party, Maigret didn't attach much importance to that. It wasn't only the shot that mattered, but what had gone before, the premeditation.

He turned to Manuel, who was smoking a cigarette with an expression of defiance on his face.

"Why, since you had organized this crime of passion, did you call your brother and take the body with him to Rue Junot?"

"That's precisely the proof that I didn't shoot. If I had shot him, I would have admitted it, because I would have

146

done it in self-defense. But since it was Line, that would be more difficult to believe. I told her to go home and I promised her I would do what was necessary."

Maigret looked at the two lovers in turn. Each one was as capable as the other of lying. Mori was a brazen character whom nothing up till then had stopped. But was Line any more sincere than he?

A croaking voice came from the corner where the Flea was sitting.

"It was he!" the voice said.

"Did you see him?"

"I heard him."

"Where were you?"

"I had followed Monsieur Maurice up to the third floor. I was hidden on the landing. At a certain moment I heard a woman's voice shouting:

" 'Well, shoot, will you! Don't you see he's going to kill me?'

"She hadn't spoken the last word when there was a shot. I ran downstairs."

There was a silence. The Flea now had a strange smile on his enormous mouth.

Manuel spoke first.

"He's lying. Maurice didn't attempt to shoot her."

"He's making it up," said Line. "No one said anything."

Maigret stood up and looked at each one in turn with a stern eye.

"Has anyone anything more to say?"

"No," grumbled Manuel.

"I repeat that he's lying," said Line.

"Janvier! Put the handcuffs on all three of them."

"But I didn't have any part of it," protested Jo, the younger Mori.

"Didn't you help your brother to dispose of the body?"

"That's not a crime."

"It's called aiding and abetting. Put the handcuffs on them."

"On me too?" yelped Line, as if she were going into hysterics.

"You too."

And Maigret, to Lapointe:

"Help Janvier to take them to the Central Police Station."

He was tired. He wanted to think of something else. He put his hat on and went down the big staircase.

Large drops of rain which made black disks on the pavement were beginning to fall.

He got to Place Dauphine, where two of his colleagues were having a *pastis*. He was tempted for a moment, then changed his mind.

"The biggest glass of beer you have," he said to the proprietor.

9

The bench to the left of Judge Bouteille's door was almost constantly occupied for three months. They had to find, in different towns in the provinces, the accomplices of the Mori brothers—and of Monsieur Maurice—in the robberies of châteaux and manor houses.

Experts had been called in, also, and in the end they had

tracked down where the furniture and paintings on Rue Ballu and Square La Bruyère had come from.

They had also found, at shady antique dealers' all over the country, things stolen by the gang.

Maigret had gone to Montmartre especially to congratulate the modest Inspector Louis.

"I only did my job," he said, blushing.

"Whenever you want you can be part of my team."

The Widower could hardly believe it. Perhaps, too, he was torn between the desire to be part of the main office, as it were, and his attachment to the Pigalle district.

The case went to the assizes in November. The matter of the châteaux would be dealt with separately and come up later.

In the witness box Line and Manuel continually tried to pass responsibility for the murder to the other.

The telephone call to the victim implied premeditation and the maximum penalty.

Judge Bouteille, in spite of his patience, was unable to decide between the two lovers, who had become deadly enemies.

When Line was in the witness box, one would hear a voice from the box of the accused.

"She's lying!"

"Be quiet."

"I tell you she's lying!"

"And I am ordering you to be silent."

The same scene was repeated when Manuel was being questioned.

The jury didn't settle the question. It condemned Manuel and Line to twenty years each, and Jo to five years.

And all three of them, leaving the courtroom, threw each other looks of hate.

The Flea had begun to telephone Inspector Louis again.